I love kids and they love me.
When the time comes, I think I'd be
a very good mother.

Becky's words echoed through Clark's mind.

Clark did not often run into women like Becky. The novelty of her spirit and innocence intrigued him, stirred something up in him.

Flawless-as-cream skin, hair that looked like the spun gold curls straight off a Christmas angel and every bit as wholesome. And she was a virgin, too. He'd stake his fortune on that fact.

That "fact" touched something in him, awakened his male protective instinct and made him feel proprietary, even though he hardly knew Becky. And any woman who did that for a man like Clark deserved due consideration.

Yes...Becky Taylor might just be exactly what he was looking for....

Dear Reader,

The end of the century is near, and we're all eagerly anticipating the wonders to come. But no matter what happens, I believe that everyone will continue to need and to seek the unquenchable spirit of love…of *romance*. And here at Silhouette Romance, we're delighted to present another month's worth of terrific, emotional stories.

This month, RITA Award-winning author Marie Ferrarella offers a tender BUNDLES OF JOY tale, in which *The Baby Beneath the Mistletoe* brings together a man who's lost his faith and a woman who challenges him to take a chance at love…and family. In Charlotte Maclay's charming new novel, a millionaire playboy isn't sure what he was *Expecting at Christmas,* but what he gets is a *very* pregnant butler! Elizabeth Harbison launches her wonderful new theme-based miniseries, CINDERELLA BRIDES, with the fairy-tale romance—complete with mistaken identity!—between *Emma and the Earl.*

In *A Diamond for Kate* by Moyra Tarling, discover whether a doctor makes his devoted nurse his devoted wife *after* learning about her past.… Patricia Thayer's cross-line miniseries WITH THESE RINGS returns to Romance and poses the question: Can *The Man, the Ring, the Wedding* end a fifty-year-old curse? You'll have to read this dramatic story to find out! And though *The Millionaire's Proposition* involves making a baby in Natalie Patrick's upbeat Romance, can a down-on-her-luck waitress also convince him to make beautiful memories…as man and wife?

Enjoy this month's offerings, and look forward to a new century of timeless, traditional tales guaranteed to touch your heart!

Mary-Theresa Hussey

Mary-Theresa Hussey
Senior Editor, Silhouette Romance

THE MILLIONAIRE'S PROPOSITION

Natalie Patrick

Silhouette
R O M A N C E™
Published by Silhouette Books
America's Publisher of Contemporary Romance

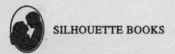

SILHOUETTE BOOKS

ISBN 0-373-19413-7

THE MILLIONAIRE'S PROPOSITION

Visit us at www.romance.net

Printed in U.S.A.

Books by Natalie Patrick

Silhouette Romance

Wedding Bells and Diaper Pins #1095
The Marriage Chase #1130
Three Kids and a Cowboy #1235
Boot Scootin' Secret Baby #1289
The Millionaire's Proposition #1413

NATALIE PATRICK

believes in romance and has firsthand experience to back up that belief. She met her husband in January and married him in April of that same year—they would have eloped sooner but friends persuaded them to have a real wedding. Ten years and two children later, she knows she's found her real romantic hero.

Amid the clutter in her work space, she swears that her headstone will probably read: "She left this world a brighter place but not necessarily a cleaner one." She certainly hopes her books brighten her readers' days.

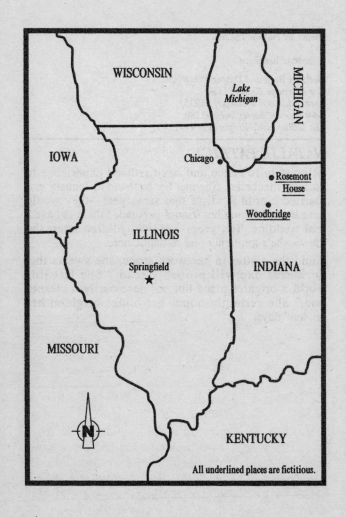

WISCONSIN

Lake
Michigan

MICHIGAN

IOWA

Chicago

Rosemont
House

Woodbridge

ILLINOIS

INDIANA

Springfield
★

MISSOURI

N

KENTUCKY

All underlined places are fictitious.

Chapter One

Why don't you just come home to Woodbridge, Indiana, meet a nice fellow, get married, get a mortgage, a minivan, and have a couple terrific kids? Becky Taylor could just hear her older brother Matt's very sensible and very predictable advice. And she wasn't taking it!

No, when she came home to Indiana, it would be in triumph. Even Matt could appreciate her need for that. Growing up—he the oldest, Becky the baby—in one of the poorest families in town, they knew what it meant to go hungry, to not know what crisis they would face next, to be scared often and sometimes angry. But they'd also known a lot of love and had been raised to believe they could do better for themselves. A lot of folks around town doubted that, but Matt had proved them wrong and so had her other brothers and sisters—now it was *her* turn.

No, she certainly would not go slinking back with

her tail between her legs after only five months in Chicago. She would not go through the struggle just to end up in another low-paying dead-end job, about the only kind a town as small as Woodbridge could provide a girl without a degree and her limited work experience.

And how could she go back and face her old boyfriend after telling him she'd outgrown the town, the life-style and most especially her puppy love/first attraction for him? The last was certainly true and had been true for most of the year they'd dated. But then how hard was it to outgrow a guy who thought buying you a microwave burrito at his father's gas station was taking you out to eat?

A guy who thought all women should be barefoot and pregnant—except when they put on their steel-toed boots to go to work at the local factory? A guy who had never understood, much less supported, her quest for self-improvement, her plans to go back to college, her longing for something more?

She shuddered. If she never saw the likes of Frankie McWurter again, it would be too soon. And if she never took her brother's typical Midwestern male advice, then...

She fingered the two tiny silver baby booties on her charm-laden bracelet, one for each of Matt's children, her niece and nephew. Thinking of her brother and his wife, Dani, and those adorable toddlers did make her think twice about never taking her brother's imagined advice. Actually, she *did* want to get married eventually and have those babies. In fact, she counted on it.

Marriage, after all, was what girls in Woodbridge,

Indiana, were raised to do best—even enlightened, educated girls, um, *women* of the so-called "Generation X." And babies? Becky loved babies, their tiny toes and fat tummies, the way they smelled, the way they cooed and laughed. The very idea of having one of her own someday radiated through her like sunshine through the dreariness of her day.

Becky absolutely wanted to get married and have a baby—with the right guy, at the right time and under the right circumstances. A triple threat, her sister-in-law would tease her and tell her the odds were stacked against realizing all three of her goals at the same time.

"Find Mr. Right," Dani would say, "and the rest suddenly won't matter quite so much."

"Find Mr. Right?" Becky muttered, clutching her thin all-weather coat close to her body. Right now she'd be happy to bump into Mr. Coffee. She stopped by the glass front of a chaotic little coffee shop on the first floor of an elegant skyscraper.

The aroma of the exotic blends, the rich lattes, the freshly ground beans all enticed her. She shut her eyes, tipped up her nose and savored it. Since savoring was all she could afford, why not enjoy the very best? she thought.

She'd checked her budget again this morning, trying to find just enough extra to allow her to replace the contact lens she'd lost the night before. She glanced at the image of herself reflected in the huge plate-glass window before her. Even her best perfect-pink job interview suit didn't make up for the pair of bent wire-framed glasses perched on her nose or the still-damp mass of golden-brown curls glommed on top of her head. If only her roommate hadn't moved out last week and taken the blow dryer along with her half of the living expenses, her hair at least might be presentable, Becky thought.

No, her budget would not budge for contacts or coffee. When she'd lost her job last week, she'd stocked the fridge and paid the rent and figured out the total cost of utilities, necessities and buying a paper every day for job-hunting purposes. Luxuries like latte did not fit in the picture.

She gazed longingly at the hot steaming cups set down by the waitress. Even the half-empty ones, which got whisked away almost before the patrons had left the premises, didn't look bad to Becky today. She fought off a yawn and moved her bedraggled umbrella from one shoulder to the other. In the shop, two women in stark business attire got up from their seats, their cups still brimming, and left the coffee disregarded as lightly as the cast-off newspaper one tossed onto the counter.

Of course! Becky brightened. If she spent her allotted money for a plain, small cup of coffee and lingered over it long enough, she could gather up someone's unwanted paper for free. Not only could she get the want ads that way but she wouldn't go through the day feeling like some job-hunting zombie.

Her heavy charm bracelet jangled and icy water droplets splashed on her wrist and leg. She yanked and pulled and finally got her miserable pink-and-blue floral umbrella shut. She looked at the sad old thing with one rib bowed out and another bent at a forty-degree angle so that even closed it seemed as if about to burst into a rendition of "I'm a little teapot." As soon as she got a job, that umbrella was going to go and the first thing she was going to buy was a new one, she told herself. No, make that the second thing.

She pushed through the heavy glass doors of the mammoth building, heading for the inner entrance to the shop. The first thing she would buy was a new charm for her bracelet—to mark the passage into this new, mature phase of her life. She gave her bracelet a confident shake and forged ahead, throwing herself into a throng of gray suits and shuffling wing tips.

Ping.

"My charm!" She'd felt the small object bounce against her knee moments before it hit the floor. A quick check of her bracelet told her she'd lost one of the baby booties she so cherished. Replacing it at a time like this was not an option, she thought. She had to find it!

She scanned the floor. The bright silver should stand out against the black marble, shouldn't it?

She raised her hand to bite her fingernail and unintentionally stabbed not one, but three passersby with the tip of her crooked umbrella.

"Sorry. So sorry. I'm sorry." She tried to meet the eyes of each of those she'd gouged.

None of them returned her gaze. She hung her head, feeling two feet tall. Of course, she thought, if she were two feet tall, at least then she might spot her charm more readily. She'd lost her job last week, her contact last night and her baby bootie moments ago, but that didn't mean she had to lose her sense of humor or her dignity.

"Oh, my!" She gasped as something metallic winked at her just a few inches from the elevator doors. Maybe she didn't have to lose her bootie after all. Disregarding the flash of feet and press of bodies, she dove for the tiny trinket, determined not to let it get swept inside the opening elevator doors.

Her teeth jarred as her knees hit the floor. Her fingers ached in stretching so hard to reach. Almost. Almost...

Crunch.

"Ow!" She drew back her hand, her fingertips smarting. The charm had disappeared and the man who had clomped on her fingers with it inside the elevator.

Scrambling to her feet, she jerked her head up in time to see a tall, black-haired man in a tailored suit and white shirt that set off the dark undertones of his skin dig something small and silver out of the heel of his shoe.

"That's my charm," she called out.

The man looked up and directly into her eyes. Her heart stopped. This was not the kind of man she normally ran into in Woodbridge or even in her usual activities around Chicago. Those kinds of men, the best of the bunch, wore power ties. This man wore power itself, raw yet refined, barely contained the way his fitted suit could not entirely temper the primitive qualities of his lean, muscular body.

His lips, pale and hard, looked like they could kiss a girl senseless, and Becky had no doubt that life provided him ample opportunity to do just that. His straight nose and dark eyebrows set off his penetrating brown eyes, which, she imagined could practically spark to telegraph underlying anger or humor or even lust.

She gulped in the damp morning air carried in on overcoats and rain hats.

Had she ever seen such compelling features, Becky thought, even in his current mild state of bewilderment? Yes, she decided with one more look, she had—in late-night movies on her thirteen-inch borrowed TV. Cary Grant, she thought. A younger, in-the-flesh version of the world's most romantic movie star had just crushed her fingers—and taken off with her baby-bootie charm. She blinked her eyes and came back to reality.

"Hey, you! You, in the expensive suit." She pointed at him with her umbrella. "You can't just grab my bootie and take off like that."

Heads turned.

She thought she heard at least one indignant huff.

She wanted to pull her coat up over her head and quietly slink away.

At the back of the elevator, the man with the Cary Grant face didn't even blink. He gave a droll smile, cocked his head above the push of people wedging into the small cubicle and shouted back, "It was an accident, miss. Rest assured, I wouldn't have *grabbed* anything of yours on purpose."

A strange little squeaking noise gurgled in the back of her throat. *Wouldn't have grabbed anything of yours...* Why that smug jerk, she thought. Of course, if he was the jerk, why was she the one who felt like running away?

She took a step backward. A lock of her already droopy hair plopped cool and wet against her scorched cheek. Her glasses wobbled. The last possible passenger stepped into the waiting elevator. The gorgeous jerk and her precious memento were about to disappear.

"I won't forget this, you know. I am not the kind of girl who lets some man—even a man like you— take her b—" She caught herself. This was obviously an important man; she needed to rise to the occasion with class and dignity. "I am not the kind of girl who lets a strange man take advantage of a situation, then just walk away without expecting some kind of accountability."

"Good for you," he told her with an almost imperceptible wink. "One rarely finds a girl willing to defend her...charms so vehemently these days."

"Oh! You..." Words simply would not do. This situation called for action—drastic, immediate action. She thrust her deformed umbrella forward between the closing doors. Unfortunately, someone inside the elevator saw it coming and batted away the protruding umbrella tip. The momentum carried it in a slow upward swing until it popped open of its own accord in all its ragged glory. As the door slid shut between herself, her charm and her living vision of masculinity and sophistication, she could only stand there looking for all the world like a pathetic Mary Poppins just flown in through a mild hurricane.

"Have you ever thought of...getting married?"

Clark Winstead glanced up from the silver bauble in his hand to his longtime confidant and generously overpaid tax accountant. Even knowing his always high-strung, slightly neurotic old pal would not appreciate the wry humor, he had to deadpan, "Why, Baxter, are you proposing?"

"Ha-ha." Baxter Davis shoved open the door marked The Winstead Corporation, International Headquarters and held it open for Clark. "But seriously, have you?"

"You know my stand on marriage." Just saying the word made Clark tense. Knowing even his close friend could not appreciate the depth of his feeling on the subject, the weight of the pain his own parents' miserable marriage had laid on his shoulders, he simply shrugged and gave a flippant reply. "It's against my principles."

"Oh, yeah, yeah. You're the product of divorced parents, the statistics don't bear out the risk factor, yadda, yadda, yadda. Big yawn." The door fell shut behind them. "But what about other advantages?"

Clark glanced around the bustling outer offices of his headquarters, his mind moving on to other things. "In this day and age, a man can avail himself of those *advantages* without the decided disadvantages of a marriage going sour."

"I was thinking about children."

The rounded toe of the small-scale baby bootie dug into the pad of Clark's thumb. He'd love to have a child, a son to carry on the Winstead name or a daughter to hold his heart in her delicate hands. "Actually, Baxter, I'd like to have an heir, or even two, but the price of getting them—marriage—is simply not one I'm willing to pay."

"As a wise old sage once said to me, 'In this day and age, a man can avail himself of those advantages without the decided disadvantages of a marriage going sour.'"

"I'm not the sort to adopt and raise a child on my

own, Baxter.'' They moved swiftly through the maze of desks and computers and such. Clark could not ignore but neither did he acknowledge the quiet fervor that accompanied his arrival. ''I'm too busy to do the job right, and why do anything, raise children above all, if you can't give it your best?''

''You could hire someone.''

''To have my children?'' The idea struck a spark in his muddled thoughts. He hired people for everything else that mattered to him—to run his businesses, tend to his homes. He even had a personal trainer to see that he kept his body in top shape, though he rarely needed the external motivation for that. He hired the best and let them share in the reward as well as the responsibility. Could he simply take that concept one step further?

''I meant hire someone to *raise* the child.''

That, too. If he found the right woman to bear his child, wouldn't it only follow that she would be the right one to raise it? Clear away the deadwood, get rid of everything that doesn't contribute to growth— that was his business philosophy. Why not apply it to this more personal but every bit as significant decision? And it would be neat, too, cutting out the messiness and pain of divorce and simply skipping ahead to the inevitable last step of any marital relationship— joint custody. If he could find the right woman, it might work.

''Well, you've certainly given me something to think about, Baxter.'' He paused outside the inner office occupied by his private secretary.

''Honestly, Clark, you'd consider it?''

''Having a child?''

"No, marriage."

"Marriage?" Clark gave a contemptuous snort. "Why should I?"

"For love, for companionship, and barring that, for tax purposes." Baxter fixed his beady gaze on his friend as if watching a bug under a microscope. "Marriage and children both provide tax benefits, you know."

Clark slid the trinket he'd been toying with into his pocket and brushed past his friend. "Haven't you heard, Mr. Davis, CPA and so forth? The rich don't pay taxes."

"Oh, I know all about the rich, my friend. I've learned from watching you up close and I can tell you this—it's been one fascinating study."

"Has it now?" Clark chuckled to himself.

Entertaining as he found his friend's long-winded observations about the misery of money and its effects on those who garner too much of the stuff, he didn't have time for it right now. Already this morning an unfortunate run-in had provided him with unfinished business and Clark hated unfinished business.

He held up his hand to silence Baxter's forthcoming diatribe, then hit his secretary's gleaming cherry desk with both palms flat, his arms braced. He narrowed his eyes to command her immediate focus.

"Miss Harriman, call the coffee shop downstairs right away and ask them if anyone there saw a young lady—" he straightened, making use of all his faculties to get an unerring description "—about this tall." He slashed his hand at his own chin level. "With a great mop of curly hair sort of stuck up on one side of her head."

Baxter scowled.

"A pair of lopsided glasses, carrying a badly bent umbrella and wearing a...what's it called?" He pointed to his wrist, then the answer hit him and he snapped his fingers. "Wearing a silver charm bracelet."

Miss Harriman, trained to act fast and not ask questions, already had the receiver in one hand and was tugging a pencil from behind her ear with the other.

"Find out if they know anything at all about her. Does she come here often? Work in this building? If nothing else, find out if anyone saw which way she went."

"Yes, sir," Miss Harriman said, and began jabbing numbers on the phone with the pencil eraser.

"Oh, and if the coffee shop doesn't have any answers, try the newsstand in the lobby."

"Yes, sir."

"And if that doesn't pan out, you might go down and see what you can learn from Henry, the fellow who gives the shoe shines."

"I will, sir. Whatever you say."

"Find her and there's a big bonus in it for you, Miss Harriman." He wrapped his knuckles on her desk and pivoted to head into his own expansive office.

"It always comes down to money with you, doesn't it?" Baxter practically nipped at his heels through the door, their footsteps dramatically hushed by the plush carpet as they entered the private sanctum of Clark's immense business domain.

"I have no idea what you're talking about, Baxter," Clark said, rolling the miniature baby bootie in his pocket between his thumb and forefinger.

"You've seen some woman, undoubtedly the object of your next conquest—"

"Conquest?" Clark smirked to himself at the outdated and ridiculous term. "You make it sound like I plan to climb on top of her, plant my flag and claim her as my personal territory."

"Well, you do, don't you? All possible sexual metaphors aside—"

"Yes, that's how I prefer my sexual metaphors, actually. On the side." Clark plunked down on his chair, the leather sighing as he settled in. He withdrew the small charm that had started the day's turmoil.

Baxter ignored the joke, which came as no surprise to Clark whatsoever. "When you see anything you want, whether it's another business or a new opportunity or a person, you've come to expect that all you have to do to get what you want is to throw money at it or them or him...or *her*. And once you've got them, you seal the deal with more money. Then you plant your flag, my friend. You plant it deep and you plant it good."

Clark cocked his eyebrow. "I had no idea my reputation for that kind of thing was so renowned."

Again, Baxter ignored the innuendo. "In business, you do it with your company name, your emphasis on employee empowerment and your fancy benefits packages."

"I should be shot."

"With your friends, you do it with loyalty and generosity, and don't forget jobs."

"I wouldn't dream of it."

"More than one poor sucker who happened to have grown up in your neighborhood or went to college with you or even some kid who used to deliver your paper, you've rewarded with a high-paying job and fat expense account, myself included." Baxter began to pace, his long, gangly legs taking him swiftly from one end of the room to the other. "You do it with charities, too. You buy them equipment and hand out grants. Why, just this week you're launching a scholarship program at our old university."

"That? I just want to give back some of the opportunities that helped me succeed. It's my way of coming full circle, of wrapping things up in a neat little package." He sat forward in his chair and pressed the buzzer on the office intercom. "Miss Harriman, any luck yet?"

"No, sir, not yet," the voice crackled back at him.

"Well, buzz me as soon as you find out anything."

"Yes, sir."

Where was that girl? How could she have just vanished like that?

"And women, too," Baxter raved on. "You do it with women. You most certainly do."

"I can't help it. I happen to like women." He sat back in his chair, glanced at Baxter and smiled. "That kind of thing is genetic, they say."

Baxter didn't even crack a smile.

Clark didn't care. His mind was elsewhere—with that girl. He could still see the look of stupefied innocence and outrage in her sparkling eyes, the tinge of red flushed over her peaches-and-cream complexion.

He glanced down at the charm. A baby bootie. A

token representing her own child? He thought not. No woman who had become someone's mother would allow herself to get so easily flustered by a seductive wordplay and a predatory glance by a stranger.

Besides, a mother who'd lost a sentimental token like that would have waited there by the elevators for him to bring it back to her. He'd tried, gotten off at the next floor and come back down, but she'd already taken off. Maybe it didn't mean as much to her as she wanted him to think. Maybe she'd expected him to offer a large remittance for damage to the trinket and when he did not offer that instantly…

"You've got it all figured out with women, too." Baxter created a flourish with his hand. "You lavish the women in your life with gifts and take them on luxurious trips and pamper and spoil them—"

"The poor dears, and I practically have to force them to accept."

"And when it's all over, do they want to scratch your eyes out? Write tell-all books about their horrific experiences? Slap you with palimony lawsuits?"

Clark started to push the intercom button again, then curled his fingers into a fist. Someone had to have seen that girl. Her appearance alone drew enough attention to her to insure that, and the scene she'd made, not to mention her last threat to him…

"No, any woman you've tangled with always wants to stay friends. They actually still like you even after you've treated them like goddesses and given them their every desire!"

"Imagine that. They must be deluded."

"Yes, they are, and the sad fact is they don't even know it."

"If you were deluded and you knew it, you wouldn't exactly be deluded, not in the strictest sense, would you?"

"They think they're happy!"

"But they're not?"

"No! How could they be? They've all been run through the Clark Winstead patented self-integrity shredder."

Clark frowned. "Which one of my companies makes that one?"

"Make fun if you want. But I'm telling you the truth. Look out this window." Baxter swiveled Clark's chair around so that he had a view of the street below. "Any other person would look at all those people there and see the pride and accomplishments, boredom and despair, the little joys and deep-seated depressions that are all part of the human condition."

Clark gazed at the smudges of color through the rain-speckled glass. She was out there, somewhere. A wounded kitten who thought her claws made her a tiger. How was he going to find her?

"But does Clark Winstead see those things? No, he does not!"

Clark scanned the bustling crowd, wondering if he might be able to pick her out from this distance.

"Clark Winstead sees every human being with a price tag on them." Baxter straightened up, his neck lengthened, his chin up. He gave his head a shake like a rooster getting ready to crow. "And if he likes what he sees, he has no problem meeting that price to get his way."

Clark blinked, then twisted his head toward his friend. "What's that supposed to mean?"

"It means that all of us, every employee who takes a frivolous bonus or accepts a bigger salary than they earnestly merit, every woman wearing a piece of jewelry given by you—and not a one of them a wedding or engagement ring in all your thirty-nine years, I might add—"

"The first few of those thirty-nine years they had to settle for candy necklaces, I'm afraid."

"Every charity that names a Clark Winstead scholarship winner or dedicates a Clark Winstead memorial wing," Baxter went on with dogged determination to finish, "every friend who takes a handout and company that gets treated to one of your affable takeovers, we're all walking around with your flag blazing over us—planted right square in our backs—like the proverbial dagger."

"I'll have to see if our insurance covers that kind of thing."

"We all know, deep down, that you've got us. We're bought and paid for and we owe you. As much as we like you, we *do* owe you. We've sold out, and no man—or woman—can be truly happy knowing that about themselves."

Clark considered that a moment.

"*That's* why I think you've never married, my friend."

"I've never married—I never intend to marry—because I do not personally believe in the institution. I saw how it destroyed my parents and I want no part of it." He started to turn his attention back toward the window.

"Ha!"

Clark gawked at Baxter.

"You've never married, Clark Winstead, ol' pal, because you know what I just said is true. You know that you could have any woman you want, but you don't want any woman you could have because in your heart you'd know it was just another sellout. Ironical, isn't it?"

"What's that?"

"That good ol' Clark Winstead is trapped in the same illusion as he's created for the rest of us. He thinks he's happy, but because of who he is and what he's got, he can't be—"

"Then I'm content in my anguish," he lied, feeling all but content in his impotence at finding this girl with the wayward charm.

"Ha!"

"What is your point, Baxter? What?" he finally snapped. Baxter had it all wrong about him. He really did bear the scars of a terrible childhood. Watching his parents squabble and then drag him into the middle of the fray made him vow that he would never go through that again. Most of all, he would never put another child through it. To hear his hidden pain made light of on top of the incident with the girl did not put him in a sterling mood. "Listening to you, a person might think I'm some kind of devil."

"Worse."

"Worse than a devil?"

"Yes, much worse because you're not just a devil…"

Suddenly, a splash of blue and pink out the window caught his eye, then the outline of an umbrella shaped like a squatty teapot. Her! She was standing there on the street corner, her head bent over her cupped palm.

"…you, Clark Winstead, are the worst kind of devil. *You* are a decent man."

"Hold that thought, will you?" Clark stood so fast his chair spun halfway around and slammed against his leg. In two long strides he was at his office door.

"Hey, where are you going?"

Clark grinned and gave the door a mighty push. "Off to corrupt another soul."

Chapter Two

"Twenty-five, thirty-five, thirty-six...forty-six..."
Becky flicked her fingernail through the change in her
hand and muttered, "Give me back my charm, that's
what I should have said."

The wind plastered her thin coat against her back.
The umbrella that balanced over her shoulder rustled
in the wind. Rain from the flapping awning overhead
splashed the back of her neck and made her shiver.
She lifted her head, suddenly on alert. People hurried
past her as if she did not exist.

In the past five months, she'd grown accustomed
to that feeling. But even after that amount of time on
her own in the city, she could not accept getting
stepped on or having something of hers so blithely
whisked away.

That arrogant jerk's attitude still galled her and if
he were here right now she'd probably... The image
of him, this virile suit-and-tie man with a super-

charged aura of confidence, to-die-for eyes and a quick, wicked grin, filled her mind.

She'd probably stare at him like the big, uncultured goof that she knew in her heart she was, she thought. Her shoulders slumped forward. Maybe her brother had the right idea. Maybe she should go back to Woodbridge, marry a guy like Frankie McWurter and have a bunch of bucktoothed kids with big ears who all looked like their hairy-backed, knuckle-dragging father.

Becky shuddered at her own meanness toward poor ol' Frankie and at the prospect of marriage to a small-town Lothario. On the other hand, she thought, maybe she'd stay in the city and give finding a job another shot. After all, after a day like today, how much worse could it get?

She inched in farther under the awning, closed her umbrella and propped it against her shin. She narrowed her gaze again over her cluster of coins. "Forty-six plus another twenty-five, that's—"

Kaching.

"Seventy-one," a deep masculine voice intoned.

"My missing charm," she whispered, raising her gaze from the slightly mangled baby bootie to the man who had just dropped it into her palm.

"No, it's my charm that's been amiss today."

Her heart did a little *kaching* of its own, skipping out an erratic rhythm at this first slow, enthralling look into that man's eyes up close. "You? You!"

"Me. Me."

"I looked all over for you in there." She pointed lamely to the building across the way. "Even got in the very next elevator to try to catch up with you."

"And I got on the very next one coming down."

"You did?"

"Of course, what did you think? That I'd tromp on your trinket and then not see that you got it back?"

She had thought exactly that. "Um, no, I—"

"I'm surprised our paths didn't cross in the building, though. I came right back and looked around for you, but you seemed to have disappeared without a trace. Instead of wasting too much time trying to seek you out, I went up to my office and had my secretary start an all-points search for you."

"Y-you did?" Wow, she thought, her and her little charm had caused all *that?*

"I did indeed. She didn't have any luck, either. Why was that? Did you take the stairs coming back down?"

"No." She lifted her face and inhaled the smell of rain and exhaust from the street mixed with just a hint of masculine cologne from his expensive overcoat. "I, um, I had no idea where you were headed, so I, kind of, well, I...I pressed every button in the elevator, and when the doors opened, I stuck my head out to see if there was any sign of you."

"I'm sure that made you very popular with the elevator crowd."

"Well, when you look slightly unbalanced, people don't tend to voice their complaints." She held out her arms a bit, offering herself as evidence.

He took a long, leisurely look at her, not the least bit hesitant in showing how his gaze traveled from the tips of her waterlogged shoes to the top of her haywire hairdo. A subtle smile played over his hard lips at the parts in between. Nothing leering, just a hint of appreciation that carried over into his voice as he said, "I think you look very nicely balanced."

She giggled. *Giggled.* That's a great way to impress a suave man like this, she chided herself.

"And I admire your character, not afraid to go after what you wanted, protecting what belonged to you, Miss...Mrs...?"

"Ms."

"Of course, how Neanderthal of me." He smiled but not just with his lips—with his eyes, the tilt of his head, the lines in his face. Even his posture added to his air of amusement. "Ms...?"

"Taylor. Becky—Rebecca—Taylor." He admired her. Who'd have expected that? She tugged off her warped glasses and shoved them into her coat pocket. Legally, she needed the corrective lenses for driving and they helped tremendously when navigating the streets of Chicago on foot, but in a pinch she could get along without them. She pulled free the rubber band constraining her ponytail, shook her head, then fluffed her hair with one hand. "Becky, usually."

"Well, Ms. Becky usually, I believe I owe you an apology for not returning this to you more promptly."

He tapped the charm in her still-outstretched palm with his blunt fingertip.

The coins jingled.

Becky's pulse leaped.

The simple gesture of this man dipping his finger into the hollow of her hand had an instant, almost erotic effect, with tiny, tingling waves building outward from the spot where his skin touched hers.

"I hope I didn't inconvenience you too much by the delay," he said.

"Oh, no. You didn't delay me. You couldn't delay me. I mean, I have nowhere special to go. Oh...that makes me sound homeless or...I'm not, not yet at least. I'm job hunting, so you see...I'm just unemploy..." The words rushed out all breathless with an unexpected young-girl quality that made her self-conscious, aware of the need to shut herself up. "Um, thank you."

"You're welcome." He took his hand away and slipped it into his pocket, but before he did, Becky took the time and care to notice that he wore no wedding ring.

She focused on the objects remaining in her hand, wanting to say something, anything, to show herself as calm and casual about the whole awkward situation. This man had seen her looking like a big fool after all, and suddenly it felt very important to counteract her first impression. She plucked up the bootie, turning it this way and that. The gray morning light brought out the flaws and fine details of its design. A thought struck her. "I feel a little like Cinderella here. You know, you tracking me down with only this shoe to go on."

"That would make me, what? Prince Charming?"

"That's Snow White. I don't think the prince in Cinderella ever gave his name." She shifted her umbrella. "See? There's another similarity. You haven't given me your name, either."

"Winstead. Clark Winstead." He extended his hand.

Clark Winstead. He even had a great name. She put her own hand forward, remembered she still held the bootie in her fingers, dropped her gaze to it, then started to tuck it back into her other hand.

Clark Winstead stopped her.

"Here, if you don't mind?" He took the trinket, apparently forgetting about the handshake entirely.

Becky felt a twinge of regret at not getting to feel her hand in his. They'd made a connection, she thought, one she'd have liked to prolong if only with a more formal introduction.

"I notice it's a bit worse for the run-in with my heel." He examined the charm with one eye half-shut, then fixed those amazing eyes on her. "Why don't you let me have my jeweler fix that for you?"

This guy has his own jeweler? she thought.

"Or I could replace it altogether," he suggested.

"Oh, I wouldn't want a new one. This one has sentimental value."

"For your own baby?"

"No, I've never had any babies." She gazed up into those heart-melting brown eyes. But I'd have yours, a little voice inside her sighed. "I do hope to have one someday."

He nodded as if she'd just confirmed something to him.

"I know I don't look terribly responsible or anything right now, but I am. I've always had goals in my life—like going to college, moving to Chicago. I made the second one happen—obviously—and hope to make the first one happen when I can afford it. I think that's the kind of thing that helps make a good mother, having priorities and never slacking off on self-improvement."

She knew she sounded like she was applying for

the job. She felt the heat rise from her neck to her cheeks, even singeing the rims of her ears, at her chattering on. But a girl like her only met a prince, or a Clark Winstead, once in a lifetime, and something inside her told her to give him as much information about herself as she possibly could. It couldn't hurt and something she said might just strike a chord in the guy.

"Plus I love kids and they love me. When the time comes, I think I'd be a very good mother."

"No doubt."

What had she thought? That he'd be so awed by her blathering that he'd propose right on the spot and ask her to bear his child? She folded her coat around her like a security blanket. "Um, in answer to your question, the bootie charm is for my nephew. I have one for my niece, too. I have a charm for every major event in my life."

She held up the bracelet before she could stop herself from the childish, bumpkin behavior. Like the man wanted to see her stupid bracelet!

"Delightful," he said. "May I?"

This time, he took her hand in his and Becky decided then and there she knew how the "real" Cinderella must have felt when the prince slid that glass slipper into place on her foot.

He turned her hand over and the bracelet clattered softly. "Why, it looks like you've led a very full life, Ms. Taylor."

"I guess as full as a girl can lead and still be allowed to sing in the church choir in Woodbridge, Indiana."

He laughed, probably just out of politeness, but it

was a warm, genuine-sounding laugh all the same that radiated through Becky's rain-soaked being.

He raised his eyes to look at her, his chin still tucked in. "That's where you're from? Woodbridge, Indiana?"

"Born and raised," she said, nodding.

"Lucky Woodbridge."

"Thank you," she whispered.

He released her hand and reached inside his pocket. In a moment, he had withdrawn two perfect business cards the color of rich vanilla ice cream. He handed them both to her, then took a pen from inside his overcoat.

Becky recognized the type of pen from window-shopping for a gift for her brother's last birthday. That simple, stylish, fine writing instrument, as they were called in the store, easily cost more than she could earn in a month at her old job in Woodbridge. Well, she thought, had she expected less from a prince?

"Write down your name, address and phone number on one of these," he said. It wasn't a request.

He wants my number, she thought. Her fingers could hardly grip the pen he handed her.

"I'll take the charm to my jeweler to be repaired, then have him send it to you."

"Oh." She blinked. The noises of the city, which had seemed muted by the very presence of the man, came rushing back to fill her ears. Car horns blared, tires whooshed over the wet road, people called out to one another. Becky swallowed hard and managed to eke out a stiff but respectful "Thank you."

If she had a shred of pride left, she'd tell him not to trouble himself. Correction—if she had pride and enough money to get the charm repaired herself, she'd tell him...

She looked up into that face.

His gaze brushed over her chin, her lips, her hair, then settled on her eyes.

She'd tell him... "Here you go. If it takes past the end of the month, I may not be at that apartment anymore, so I jotted down my brother's address in Woodbridge."

He slid the card slowly from between her fingers and placed it in his breast pocket. "Good. And you keep my card just in case they don't do the job to your satisfaction."

She ran her fingertip over the engraved lettering. "Thank you. I will."

He tipped his head and took a step backward. "Goodbye, then."

"Bye." She smiled, then stepped back herself, bumping into a burly mailman as she did. Her umbrella slid down her shin and clunked to the pavement, rolled into the gutter, then burst open just in time to get run over by a speeding taxi.

She was having one of the worst days of her life and the only prince she'd ever meet was right there to witness it.

Becky Taylor was either the sweetest, most innocent young woman he had ever run across—or she was a stark, raving lunatic.

"Miss Harriman, have this sent to my regular jeweler for repair and then have it..." He glanced down at the name and number written in delicate swirls on the back of one of his business cards.

Plus I love kids and they love me. When the time

comes, I think I'd be a very good mother. Her words echoed through his mind.

He ran his thumb along the sharp edge of the card.

Flawless-as-cream skin, hair that looked, when not bunched up on her head, like the spun-gold curls straight off a Christmas angel and every bit as wholesome.

Clark did not often run into girls like that. The novelty of her spirit and innocence intrigued him, stirred something up in him. Other things about her stirred him up, as well.

Not too thin, but not too plump, either, the girl had a body that would fill a man's hands, that could fulfill his most primal fantasies. Not like those stick-figure women who inhabited his moneyed world. That type wouldn't do more than nibble on the exorbitant meals he'd buy them at all the best restaurants, but they'd damn sure eat a girl like Becky Taylor alive if given the chance.

And she'd give them indigestion for their trouble, too, he decided with a wry smile.

He chuckled to recall the fury she'd shown when she thought he'd made off with her prized ornament. Oh, sure, she looked like a pitiful but precious rag doll at first glance, but underneath it she had fire in her, self-reliance and character. And she was a virgin, too. He'd stake his fortune on that fact.

That "fact" touched something in him, awakened his male protective instinct and made him feel proprietary even though he hardly knew the girl. And any girl who did that to a man like him, someone suspicious of entanglements since childhood and distanced from them by choice in adulthood, deserved due consideration.

Yes—provided she wasn't a lunatic—Becky Taylor might just be exactly what he was looking for.

He closed his hand over the crisp card. "Just have the charm repaired, Miss Harriman, then returned to me. I think I can handle it from there."

Chapter Three

A hot shower. A cool drink. A warm bed, then out cold. That's all Becky wanted tonight. Feet aching and spirit sagging, she trudged up the first flight of stairs, with their worn rubber surface, to her tiny apartment. She gripped the wobbling handrail for support and clutched a file folder filled with copies of her résumé, job applications and the day's paper, thinking only of the night ahead. Well, not *only* of the night ahead, she corrected herself, rounding the first landing. One other thing she wanted, and wanted badly—to put Clark Winstead completely out of her mind once and for all.

She hadn't done that last night or the night before. In fact, not one morning or afternoon or evening or night—since she'd met the man three days ago—had gone by without something reminding her of him. Each morning when she closed the clasp on her favorite charm bracelet before going out job hunting, she thought of him. When she'd spent an afternoon on a temp job handing out samples of expensive men's cologne, she thought of the scent that had clung unobtrusively to his overcoat. In the evening, when she enjoyed the only entertainment she could afford— a romance novel checked out from the library—the hero's voice became his voice in her mind. And when she went to sleep at night...

Becky bit her lip and staggered to a stop on the second landing. Such dreams! And from a former vacation Bible school assistant teacher and onetime Sweetheart of the Future Farmers of America! She blushed at her own imagination in an area that had, until now, not been overly explored in her life. In aspects of romantic love and unbridled lust, Becky could count herself a novice, a subnovice, in anything approaching serious intimacy. Quaint and old-fashioned as it probably seemed to many, she'd always figured she would reserve learning more about "it" until after she got married.

Now, one bumbling run-in with Clark Winstead and she seemed ready to sign up for night school! What had become of her? She laughed to herself at the ridiculous idea that a man like Winstead would even recall who she was, much less want to sign on as her very own professor of passion.

She started up the stairs again with renewed vigor. This wasn't the mopey little farm girl who had arrived in Chicago months ago. She had too much at stake here to let childish fancies, or even mature fantasies, distract her from her real work of finding a job and making it on her own. She did not need a man to come along and make everything wonderful for her.

She had everything it took to make her own way in life, to succeed and excel. She hardly needed rescuing, for heaven's sake. She was strong and resourceful and determined; those traits alone would see her through this current crisis in good stead.

Forget the fairy tales, she told herself, where the prince sweeps the ragamuffin girl off her feet and into a magical world of romance and riches. That kind of thing never happened in the real world. And Becky, with her temp job over and her prospects for gainful employment about as bleak as the overcast evening skies, lived dead center in the real world.

She would probably never see her would-be Prince Charming again, except in her dreams. That, she decided as she took the last step of the dreary four-story walk up to her small apartment, was the story of her life. No job. No prince. No—

"Clark!"

Clark jerked his head up to find a pair of beautiful, shock-widened eyes fixed on him. He stiffened from his jaw to his work-tightened shoulders and all points southward. *All* points.

That this woman had that kind of intense physical effect on him puzzled and disturbed Clark only slightly more than the profound protectiveness he had felt toward her at their very first meeting. Something about this woman penetrated his steely control and got right to the core of his being. He did not like that. Did not like it one bit.

Clearing his throat, he forced himself to relax as much as he could in this circumstance and give her a smile of indulgent benevolence. "Hello again."

"Hello." Ms. Taylor looked as if she wanted to say more, to say anything, but no sound came out.

Clark did not mind. He enjoyed watching her full lips part, purse, then open slightly. Then, seductive in the sheer instinct of the action, her tongue flicked out to brush the center of her lower lip. Clark found himself wishing he could do the same—brush his tongue slowly, instinctually, over those lips and then—

Becky blew out a long, breathy whistle and shook back her hair.

She wanted him to kiss her, he reasoned. He looked into her eyes and felt them practically pleading for it.

She blinked. "Clark. It's really…it's really you."

"Yes, it is." He stepped toward her. Really him. Really just about to fulfill the inner need he saw in her, beckoning to him. He angled his head downward just enough to put him in position and then, when her mouth opened again—

"Wh-what on earth are *you* doing *here?*" She plunked her hands on her hips and gaped at him.

The stinging disbelief of her tone slapped him back to his senses. He stepped back, unsure of what to say to her. After all, Clark had asked himself the same question—what on earth *was* he doing here?

He'd asked himself that question more than once today already: when he'd put a senior VP on hold to take a phone call from the jeweler, again when he'd made specific arrangements that the charm not be left with a secretary but delivered to him personally, and yet again when he'd cut short a meeting to take the time to bring the charm to Ms. Taylor himself.

He glanced around at the dimly lit hallway lined with brown-painted doors with brackish brass numbers on the frames. It wasn't a shabby place by any means, clean but unremarkable, not at all the kind of place he'd have chosen for Becky, though. "Actually, I was just thinking the same thing myself."

"You were?"

"Yes, I was wondering what a girl like you was doing living in a place like *this.*" He'd asked it to turn things back to his advantage, he thought, but even he didn't quite believe that the question had not come from some genuine concern for her well-being. "Not that it's not perfectly...acceptable, but—"

"But?" She folded her arms over her chest, her eyes sparking with challenge.

That spark set off its own little fire in Clark. No one challenged him—not the big man, the boss, the one who signed the paychecks. He gritted his teeth to keep from grinning in sheer delight at rising to the forgotten feeling. "But I thought I'd find you living somewhere more suited to your personality."

"Like where?" The tendrils of her hair quivered with the quick, controlled jerk upward of her head. "The armory?"

Clark laughed. It felt good to laugh and really mean it. "Actually, I had more in mind the country, but I assume if you are going to insist on city life, you could do the least damage at an armory. That or one of those steel-and-marble skyscrapers with...no, no, far too many opportunities for elevator mishaps there."

"I can afford this place—at least for a while longer still. It's clean, convenient and safe. That's why *I'm* here." She tacked on a look that reminded him he had yet to explain his own presence in her building.

Clark sighed. He had no business being here, he told himself as he skimmed his thumb over the velvety box in his pocket. Damaged charm or not, he had other, far more serious responsibilities demanding his attention right now.

His mind went over the reports his legal team had handed him in the meeting he'd abandoned in favor of this errand. The operation he'd been determined to buy out, a struggling, privately owned company that would flounder within a year on its own—or flourish as a part of Clark's empire—would not sell. That incomplete transaction gnawed at his insides, but then, so had this dangling bit of unfinished business concerning a certain young lady and a bent baby bootie.

That's why he had come here today, he knew. Once he'd tidied up this nagging loose thread that was Miss Becky Taylor, his mind would settle back on his work and turn to the more pressing issues facing him. All he had to do was hand the young woman her repaired charm, wish her well in her life and then get back on track with his own life.

Clark lifted his head. His gaze honing in on Becky Taylor as a whole package now, he looked with a more critical eye to guard against any of those impulsive, wayward reactions his body might have to her. Even in the grim lighting of the vacant hallway, she looked decidedly pulled together, youthful, healthy, radiant. Her hair, caught up in some kind of casually stylish contraption that matched her blue-and-white suit, gleamed in the yellowed light from overhead. And she was not wearing those bedraggled eyeglasses that made her look as if she needed someone to take her by the hand and help guide her through the perils of life. Still, Clark found himself wishing he could take her hand just the same.

He scowled for no one's benefit but his own. He had to get this over with so he could get his mind back onto the pending buyout with all its pitfalls and problems. He coughed and then put on his most congenial, yet formal tone. "Actually, Ms. Taylor, I am, in fact, here to see you."

"I thought so. Why else would a man like you be in a place like this? It's an okay place, of course, but it doesn't exactly have Clark Winstead written all over it." She blinked at him. Her hand flattened just above her full breasts, and her cheeks flooded with a pale blush.

Any thoughts Clark had of mishandled meetings and arrested acquisitions faded on the spot.

"I mean, that is, *Mr.* Winstead."

She cocked her head.

"Yes?" He tipped his head to mimic the angle of hers. "What is it, Ms. Taylor?"

"What is what?" she whispered as if hypnotized.

"What is it you want?" He lowered his voice to match hers.

"Want? Want? I don't want anything. You're the one who came here to my apartment to see me, not the other way around." She rolled her eyes and shook her head. Twice she made a quick, gasping sound, one of exasperation that he would even ask such a thing, he believed.

"But you said my name," he reminded her.

"I did? Oh, yes, I said…" She winced, overplaying it with great zeal and apparent self-deprecating humor. "I was correcting myself—for calling you by your first name. I really shouldn't have, not without your asking me to for real, that is, not just in my..." She bit her lip, smiled and then waved one hand in the air. "Anyway, it was rude and I'm sorry."

"Think nothing of it." Clark could not think of any woman, either known to him in business or in his private life, who would have reacted so openly, so honestly, so overtly. In fact, she could not have been less subtle in her flustered chagrin, Clark decided, feeling his smile grow from practiced gesture to genuine enjoyment, if she were choking on a chicken bone. And that endeared her all the more to him. He extended his right hand. "Please, do call me Clark."

"Clark," she repeated. Her gaze sank into his, shining with blatant admiration, he assumed, and hoped he wasn't too big-headed for making that assumption. Her small hand became a perfect fit inside his larger one. Her fingers curled around his and she lowered her chin just enough that her lashes created an enticing veil over her pupils as she murmured, "And you can call me—"

"Rebecca," he concluded, wanting to let her know he had not forgotten how she had first introduced herself. Clark was a detail man and he had no compunction in letting everyone involved with him know that up front. Not that Miss Rebecca Taylor was in any way now—nor was she ever likely to be—*involved with him.* He released her hand. "Or is it Becky?"

"Becky is fine, thank you." She tucked her hands behind her back, then folded them in front, then let them fall to her sides. "I'm sorry again about calling you by your first name like that. It was so presumptuous of me, but after our little run-in, I just sort of thought of you as...well, I just sort of thought of you as a Clark and not a—" she made a dour face *"—Mr. Winstead."*

"Well, I am pleased to see I did leave a...lasting impression on you." He let his gaze linger in hers until she looked away. "And happy to report the impression my heel left on your silver charm was not quite so everlasting."

He dipped into his pocket and pulled out the box, offering it to her the way one might tempt a high-strung pony with a sugar cube—the box resting in the center of his outstretched hand.

"Why, thank you. You really didn't have to do this, you know. Just sending it back to me would have been enough."

Enough for her, perhaps, but Clark needed to see this thing safely and satisfactorily through to the end. Or so he told himself. That's why he had gone to such great lengths to return the trinket.

"Or I could have come down to your office and picked it up myself."

"No. I don't mind doing it, really." Besides, the idea of this woman loose in his office with her lethal umbrella, her pointedly honest opinions and...those great big angel eyes... Clark blinked at the turn of his thoughts, then shook his head, half-expecting to hear his suddenly short-circuited brain rattling. Even after doing it, he realized he could think of worse things than having Becky in his office, much worse—like perhaps never seeing her again.

She took the box, and just as her fingers brushed his palm, he closed his hand.

She raised her questioning gaze to his but said nothing.

He pressed the pads of his fingertips to her skin, the box still between them. Once he let go, he would have no reason to see her again—unless he made a reason. The picture of Becky dressed, as he could provide for her, in extravagant jewels and designer clothes, or perhaps in just the jewels without the clothes—sprang to mind.

Why not? Why not ask her out, set her up in a nice apartment, give her charge accounts, take her to the finest restaurants, show her the world? It might be a fun diversion for both of them for a while, until it played itself out as those things always did—always. Clark placed his other hand beneath hers and narrowed his eyes, fully prepared to make the spontaneous and quite magnanimous, to his way of thinking, proposal.

Proposition, he corrected mentally. He was not making a proposal; he was making a proposition. Plain and simple. The distinction might be subtle, but it was very real, especially with someone like Becky.

He studied the open expectation on her face, the way she looked up at him and in so doing looked up *to* him. He drew in the smell of the comfortable old building and the apple aroma of the young woman's shampoo, which seemed to so suit her. This was not the kind of girl a man propositioned—not unless he wanted a sharp, well-deserved slap in the face. He relinquished her hand.

"Um, thanks. Thank you." She curled the box close to her chest and smiled up at him without even inspecting the charm.

She trusted him. It showed in her action and in her eyes and it clawed at Clark's conscience.

"Would you...would you like to come inside?" She tossed a glance back over her shoulder at a glum brown door, a vine wreath, dotted by pink and white flowers, framing the blackened brass peephole. "It's nothing fancy, but I can fix you up some hot tea. I just made some chocolate chip cookies last night, and lucky you, I didn't quite polish them all off yet."

Lucky me indeed, he thought, to have a chance to share tea and homemade cookies with Becky Taylor. Lucky her that he could not—would not—take her up on that offer. "No thank you. I really have to get going. I have to get back to the office to see if my legal team has made any progress on an acquisition."

"Gosh, that sounds important."

He nodded. "We've been trying to convince a locally successful perfume manufacturer to sell to us so we can take his line international."

"Oh, please don't even say the word 'perfume.'" She placed her hand to her forehead and feigned reeling at the thought. "I've spent the past two afternoons on a temp job in a perfume department, and at this point I'm ready to throw every scent I own out the window and wear nothing but good old Ivory soap and baby lotion for the rest of my days."

The suggestion of Becky in nothing but soap and baby lotion prickled at Clark's sensibilities, but he forced his focus back on business. "Yes, well, I'm afraid if this manufacturer turns down my last offer, he'll be throwing his last red cent out the window. Our surveys show they'll be broke inside a year if they don't do something to shore up their finances and do it immediately.''

"Then why won't he sell to you?"

"Afraid he'll lose the personal touch that he values so much," Clark said, not in a condescending way but as a matter of fact.

"And you've tried to convince him he won't lose the personal touch by sending around a— What did you call it?—a *legal team* to deal with him?'' She shook her head. "Who'd have thought a guy conscientious enough to come around to return a silver charm in person would make *that* kind of mistake?''

In his defense, Clark reasoned, the owner of the perfume company did not look like Becky, but that was no excuse for the blatant tactical error she had just pointed out to him. "Why, Becky my dear, you are absolutely right.''

She bit her lip and grinned at the same time.

It was not that adorable sight, however, that urged Clark to ask, "What are you doing right now?"

"Um, nothing…I—''

"No plans for the evening?" It was strictly a business query, Clark told himself even though he felt a twinge of anxiety wondering if she might have a date.

"Nope. No plans. None whatsoever.''

His heart lightened.

"Why?" She eyed him with extreme caution.

"Because, in a matter of minutes, you have honed in on my fatal logical flaw regarding this deal and brought it to my attention without the irritating flattery and hemming and hawing most people usually employ with me. I like that.''

"Well, thanks. I think.''

"What's more, I need it."

"Really?"

"Really."

She scowled and folded her arms, trying not to look too pleased with his appreciation, he surmised. "And just how is it you *need* me, Mr. Winstead?"

"I thought you were going to call me Clark."

"I think that may just encourage the wrong ideas you seem to have about me, Mr. Winstead."

"Ideas?" He'd had them, no argument, but just how did she know that? Had his whole facade and business persona so completely slipped around this woman?

"I may just be a girl from a small town, but don't kid yourself, I am not some starry-eyed fool who goes all gaga over a rich, powerful man with broad shoulders and a face like..." She clenched her teeth, then cleared her throat, her gaze darting away, then back again. "I am not a fool who would just fall for a man's line, no matter how sophisticated that man might be. We have wolves in Woodbridge, Indiana, too, you know."

He laughed a deep, heartfelt laugh at her brutal honesty. "I am sure you do, my dear. I'm sure you've encountered your fair share of them, too."

"What's that supposed to mean?"

Two can play at honesty, he thought. Even as the thought of "playing" at honesty tweaked at him, he went on, giving her enough detail to let her know what he had in mind without revealing every questionable thing that had gone on in his mind to reach this conclusion. "It means you handle yourself very well. Which is why I want to ask you to accompany me on this business call I have to make—to the perfume manufacturer—if you think you can stand the scent of it just a while longer.''

"The perfume...but why?''

"To make sure I don't make any other glaring mistakes in handling the deal in person—as per your suggestion.''

She gasped, her eyes brightening. "You mean you're giving me a job?''

Clark frowned. He had thought of it more as a favor but given their economic disparities and his own desire to keep this on a professional level, he had to admit that once again the young lady had come up with a far more appropriate solution. "Yes, I am. A temporary position, granted, but you will be generously compensated for it. What do you say?''

"W-well...'' She fingered the collar of her simple blue-and-white suit. "Would I have to change?''

Clark felt a smile slowly creep over his face with pure pleasure in the moment and the sight of her standing there, all innocence and honesty. "Don't you dare, my dear. Don't you dare.''

"Well, I have to say that if this is indicative of the way you intend to handle our product from now on, I am very pleased. Very pleased indeed.'' The man they had come to do business with, Raymond McCain, spoke to Clark, but his gaze remained on Becky.

She squared her shoulders without even attempting to conceal her pride. She'd done a good job acting as corporate conscience and liaison between Clark and the common man. Though how much a man who owned his own fragrance company qualified as "common" she wasn't sure. She only knew that next to Clark, McCain seemed like a dear old grandfatherly type, sweet and unassuming, like someone she might have known back in Woodbridge. Whereas Clark—Clark was unlike anyone she'd ever met anywhere.

She'd done a good job all right, but she held no illusions that she was the reason this deal had gone through. McCain needed to sell his business and Clark wanted to buy it. She imagined there weren't many things that Clark wanted that he did not get—eventually.

Becky smiled at McCain, thinking about his story of how he had nursed the family business through thick and thin until he simply could not take it any further. McCain conceded he liked the idea of selling his treasured company to become a part of the Winstead holdings. Clark Winstead with his money, power and vision could take the company…

She glanced over at Clark, noting his chiseled jawline and just the hint of a dimple creasing his tanned cheek. He lifted his hands, large hands with blunt fingers that were impeccably kept but not manicured, to straighten his dark blue tie. He shifted his shoulders like a cat just after the kill—relaxed, yes, but still on guard. He lowered his chin, then raised just his eyes to catch her gaze.

A shiver ran through her and she fought to keep from easing out a soft sigh. Clark could take her—*it,* she corrected—he could take McCain's business *anywhere.*

"I'm very glad we came to an understanding." Clark shook the older man's hand in a quick, firm

gesture that seemed triumphant without giving the
feeling he was gloating over that triumph. "I think
our lawyers can handle it from this point, though,
don't you?"

"Our...uh...oh, oh, yes." McCain's eyes sparkled
with mischief that belied the white hair on his head.
"Let's let the lawyers do their work. That's what we
pay them for and it's obvious you have...more pressing things to get to tonight, Winstead."

Becky opened her mouth to protest, to explain that
she had come strictly as a business arrangement. The
implication that she and Clark might have any other
kind of involvement gave her gooseflesh, but it was
a lie.

Fabrications and fantasies of a better life, of dreams
and schemes about to come to fruition, of being something more than your own reality, were the fabric of
her childhood. Her father had handed them out to
Becky and her siblings the way some fathers pulled
out sticks of chewing gum from their suit pockets
upon coming home from a hard day at the office. She
would not indulge herself in that kind of thing. She
would not allow herself to believe that there could
ever be anything more than a working relationship
between her and Clark.

"Oh, Mr. McCain, I think you've got—"

"You've got the right idea, sir." Clark slapped the
older man soundly on the back. "More pressing issues indeed. I haven't eaten dinner, and neither has
Ms. Taylor. Have you, Becky?"

"Well, I...um, no."

"Good." Clark gave a sharp nod. "I think I know
just the place for a celebration."

He placed his arm over her shoulders, and for an instant Becky wondered how to read the gesture. Possessiveness? A romantic advance? Or just pleasant camaraderie?

"Won't you join us, McCain?"

Ah, she thought, camaraderie, one of the boys, business associates marking the end of the deal.

"No, thank you, Winstead." McCain gave a low, knowing chuckle. "We're done with our bargaining for the evening. Looks like it's time for you two to move on to other more interesting compromises and concessions."

Becky gasped.

McCain gave her a sly wink.

"Let me assure you, Mr. McCain." Clark's hand gripped her upper arm. His voice came low and steady, without a trace of humor but also without sounding superior, rather like a man stating a clear and irrefutable fact. "Ms. Taylor will not be compromised in the least, not tonight, and certainly not by me."

Clark turned her toward the door. But she could not resist one last glare at the older man over her shoulder. Still, even while her eyes were flashing a prim and proper "so there" to McCain's innuendo and Clark's resounding denial, something in her sank. And as she shuffled off toward the door and whatever else the evening held in store for her and this gorgeous man, she did find herself pouting just a bit at the idea that Clark did not even seem to want to compromise her, not even a little bit.

Chapter Four

"**Y**ou were brilliant with Mr. McCain, Becky." Clark slid into the taxi. He barked out his office address to the driver, then settled into the seat, trying not to crowd Becky too much with either his body or his enthusiasm.

One thirty-minute ride to the office and he would close the file on his association with Becky Taylor and call it a success. He did not want to do anything to jeopardize the delicate outcome now that it had been so neatly tied up for him.

Still, he had to make sure she knew how much he had appreciated what she had done for him tonight. "You said exactly what needed to be said, with no beating around the bush or waste of words. Just brilliant."

She leaned back against the seat and gave a short little snort in reply.

The response, from any other person on the planet,

would have startled him at the very least and sounded dismissive and boorish at the worst. Not that anyone else would have ever reacted openly like that to him, of course, which might explain why he found Becky's ingenuous scoffing refreshing to the point of being charming.

"Brilliant? Me?" She shook her head and her golden-brown curls trembled around her face. "All I did was talk to him out of my own experience as an average, everyday American consumer. Nothing brilliant there."

"Well, I certainly couldn't have done it."

"That's because there's nothing average or everyday about you," she half muttered under her breath, then catching herself, she gasped. "I mean that in a good way, of course."

"How else?" He smiled just a bit and, seeing that his smile made her even more uneasy, couldn't help but smile just a bit more.

"It's not like you could speak from the same kinds of experiences as me, that's all. It's not like you've ever had to take a job hustling perfume samples in a department store all day, have you?"

"Not that I recall. But let's not count out the possibility that I've suffered selective amnesia and entirely blocked the incident from my memory," he teased.

"Yeah, right." She laughed.

He liked making her laugh.

"I think it's pretty safe to say you are not the type who has had to schlepp himself home in a cloud of women's perfume at the end of the day."

"No, that's more likely to happen to me at the end of the *night*."

Her eyes flashed in instant recognition of the implications of his remark. This time, she did not laugh.

Well, he wasn't about to back down from the truth, he thought, not even for a girl like Becky—especially not for her. What was she to him anyway? Just a young woman who probably had far more business being back in Indiana in a cottage with a hubby and two point five kids than she did in a taxicab in Chicago with him.

Obviously, she had developed a bit of a crush on him during what had been kept plainly a business association, but was that his fault? And, yes, she had done a good job for his company, too. But she meant nothing more to him, nothing else. Why shouldn't he be open with her about his life, women's perfume and all? He looked at Becky, with her large eyes fixed on him, and suddenly he felt as though he'd kicked a puppy.

So he wasn't going to back away from the truth, but he supposed he could divert her attention from it a bit. "But you do have a point. I think if I had ever *schlepped* anything anywhere at any time, it would have clearly stuck in my mind. Tell me, did you learn a word like that back on the farm?"

"No. I learned it from Mrs. Mendlebaum across the hall." There was that smile again.

Clark tried not to enjoy it too much. He failed.

"She sort of likes to look out for me."

"Who?"

"My neighbor."

"Ah, Mrs. Mendlebaum." A stickler for details, a

man like him would not normally have made such an obvious slip. Where was his mind tonight?

"And for the record, I've never lived on a farm."

Two strikes, he thought. "I guess you just have that look about you."

"Like I've gotten up too many mornings before dawn to milk the cows? Or like I've spent my days knee-deep in pig slop?" She raised an eyebrow, her eyes dancing with the challenge for him to wiggle his way out of that one. Then wet her lips like a woman waiting to be kissed, tempting him in an obvious way to either "put up or shut up."

"Neither." Clark leaned forward, answering that challenge with a closeness that carried a warning not to tempt him too much unless she intended to follow through. "You look like a girl a man would want to stretch out with in the hay and kiss half-senseless until those lips of yours were swollen from the passion and straw clung to your golden hair and..."

He cut himself off. He'd gone too far. What had started as a lesson to her had shifted to a study in why he should not let his guard down around this woman.

While the traffic around them slowed to a crawl, he found his pulse racing. Becky did things to him no other woman could, and it wasn't just a case of white-hot lust, either. In fact, if Clark was going to label it—and he wasn't—he'd call it just about anything but lust. He wanted her, no denying that, but he also wanted more from her than some meaningless coupling and a sophisticated parting of the ways when the hormonal rush wore off.

If he believed for even the slightest moment that something like love existed, he'd say that this was something like that. Not a full-blown case, but the first stirrings, he supposed. *If* there were such a thing, he reminded himself. No, something else was at work here, something Clark wanted to know more about before he let it—and the woman who inspired it— walk out of his life forever.

Becky fidgeted with her purse, then tugged at the edge of her suit jacket even though it lay perfectly in place. She wet her lips again. She looked at Clark, then darted her gaze away.

A gentleman, he supposed, would say something to alleviate her discomfort. But around Becky, Clark did not want to be a gentleman, and for that very reason he had to fight doubly hard to be exactly that.

He sat back in the cab and inhaled its dank odor. "As I said before, you did a good job with McCain, and when we get back to my office I'll make sure you are well compensated for the work."

"I just spoke my mind, Clark." She drew her shoulders up. "Gee, if I'd known that someone could get well compensated for *that,* I'd be as rich as…well, as rich as you are."

And worth every penny, he thought.

"But really, I can't accept a lot of money from you for this. It wouldn't be right."

No, he amended, hers was a treasure beyond any mere price.

She opened her hands in a dismissive gesture. "I didn't *do* anything, really."

"Didn't do anything?" This time, he made that strange little snorting sound and found it quite satis- fying. "You set me on the right path to making this deal happen. A dozen lawyers and who knows how many financial advisers had failed to make that kind of breakthrough before you. I should reward you handsomely.''

''That's silly, really. For what? For pointing out the obvious?''

''Yes, that. And you enchanted McCain.''

''Enchanted?'' A car horn blared somewhere behind them as if to underscore her shock at the term. ''Is that what they call it in Chicago?''

Their driver swerved just enough to jostle them against one another. Clark savored the faint scent of the perfume McCain had insisted she dab on her neck.

Becky pulled away, lifted her head and straightened up prim as a schoolmarm beside him. ''Back home in Woodbridge, we have another name altogether for how Mr. McCain acted.''

''And what's that?''

''A dirty old man.'' She narrowed her eyes and Clark couldn't help doing the same. ''Really! The way he leered at me when he said all that about compromises and concessions. You don't have to have been born in a city or come home wearing someone else's perfume at night to guess what was on his mind.''

''I know exactly what was on McCain's mind, Becky.'' The same kinds of things had run through Clark's mind all evening. ''Does that make me a dirty young man?''

She waved off the notion with one delicate hand. ''Don't be silly.''

''I'm never silly. It was just my way of letting you know that I—''

''That you can think like McCain doesn't make you

a dirty young man.'' She cut him short with a no-nonsense glare. ''You're not *that* young.''

''You aren't going to let me get away with anything, are you?''

''Remember that and we'll do fine.''

''Yes, I think you're right.'' Suddenly, Clark understood what it was he felt for her. Not single-minded lust or a sham of an emotion some people called love. He felt for her the one thing he valued most from his friends and associates. Finally, after years and years of pleasant enough relationships, filled with fun and companionship but little else, Clark had met a woman who did not want any more from him than what he was willing to give her.

He respected that about Becky Taylor and he wasn't going to let go of that lightly. Clark gave her an approving nod.

Becky returned the man's gesture, her expression cocky to cover up the sheer panic she felt just beneath the surface of her facade. You are out of your depth, Becky girl, her mind raged. She had to cut this out and get herself back to the real world right now before she ended up with a broken heart—and who knows what other damaged parts—to show for the encounter.

''Gee, the traffic sure is bad this evening,'' she said, trying to direct the conversation to a way out for herself.

''The closer we get to the office it should start to thin out,'' Clark assured her.

''I thought we were going to celebrate the deal.'' Celebrating anything with Clark suddenly seemed a bad idea, but that wasn't the kind of thing she could just blurt out and make a scene. Especially since she had noticed the driver's furtive glances at them ever since Clark made those remarks about her and the hay.

She bit her lip just thinking of how his warm, husky voice had made the whole image so forbidden yet so inviting. She touched her fingertips to the base of her throat and let her gaze flicker away. In doing that, she caught the cabbie's eye in the rearview mirror. The knowing glimmer she saw there yanked her back to the moment and her goal of getting this over with and getting on with her dull but very real life.

"If we're going to celebrate, then let's just get to it," she whispered, finding that her own tension brought an emphasis to each word and amplified them in the cramped confines of the cab. "I really don't see why we have to go to your office first."

"Well, if we don't go to the office, how am I going to give you your money?"

"Money!" Becky swore she heard the cabdriver snicker. She lowered her voice and her head to shut out any further eavesdropping. "I told you I didn't want any money. I didn't do anything but be myself—oh, and get leered at. Back in Woodbridge, we also have a name for a girl who takes money for getting leered at."

"And I'm guessing that name is *not* Mrs. Mendlebaum."

"No." She glowered at him and hoped he didn't know how hard she had to concentrate to keep from laughing out loud at the picture of Mrs. Mendlebaum as a woman of questionable repute.

"No. No. I didn't think so." He shook his head. "So, what you're telling me is that even though you originally agreed to come with me as my…personal consultant…"

The driver snorted at the choice of title.

Clark leaned back, his shoulders taking up half the space in the cab, it seemed. "…you are now saying that you won't accept payment for your services?"

The snort turned into a chortle. Becky had always wondered what a chortle would sound like, but the second that smarmy, guttural sound came from the front seat she knew for certain that was one.

"I'm saying—" she raised her voice as much for the benefit of the driver as to drive her point home with Clark "—that once I got there I realized I *didn't do anything* that deserved any money."

"Now, don't sell yourself short—"

"I didn't sell myself at all. You did something nice for me by bringing me my charm in person. I did something nice for you by acting as a buffer while you negotiated a business deal." She whisked her hands together as if wiping them off. "Done and done. You wash my back, I wash—"

"Sounds promising. Please go on." Clark grinned.

She could lose herself in that grin, in those eyes, in this fantasy. But how long would it last and how much would she really lose? She'd already lost most of her childhood to dreams that never came true. She did not want to risk another moment.

"I wash my hands of all of this. I think maybe you just better take me home."

"I'm sorry but I can't do that."

"Why not?"

"Because if I take you home now without repaying

you for what you've done, there'll be unfinished business between us again.''

"I can live with that.''

"Well, I can't. So, you have to at least let me take you out to eat. To do something to say thank-you for your help tonight.''

He wanted to take her out to eat. Visions of four-star restaurants, of champagne and tuxedoed servers and food so rich she'd have hiccups for a week, filled her imagination. Only the hiccup part seemed real, she decided. And she needed real.

So Clark Winstead wanted to square things up with the little match girl who did him a favor. Well, that was just fine and dandy, Becky thought. But he would have to do it on her turf, not off in a land of milk and money where she could never fit in, where she would find herself more hungry for all the things she could not have after the meal than before.

"My small-town morals won't let me accept your brand of repayment. Your personal ethics won't let you walk away without doing something. How about a compromise?''

"And you said McCain was a dirty old man for even suggesting such a thing.'' He burned his gaze into her, his eyes hooded, and wearing just enough of a smile to bring out his dimple. "I'm all ears—well, not all of me—but since you claim you've already washed my back, I suppose you know that.''

"I know....'' She knew he wasn't all ears—he was all man. Even sitting in a cab with him, with a nosy driver in front, the droning, endless traffic surrounding them and her own defenses on red alert, nothing could dampen the masculine energy that seemed to shimmer all around him.

Rich. Sexy. Funny. Charming. Fair. What a jerk, she thought. Why couldn't he have left her alone with just her dreams about him? Why did he have to show up and prove to her how far out of reach a man like that was for a girl like her?

She gritted her teeth. The sooner she got this over with, the sooner she could put this man out of her mind forever. "I know that you want to thank me. Then why don't you thank me the way a fellow from my hometown would? Take it or leave it, that's my offer."

"I'll take it." He said it as if the whole thing had been his idea all along. Strong and forceful without even a trace of hesitation.

As Becky smiled to herself and gave the driver new directions, she had to wonder if Clark would feel so confident if he knew where their evening was going to end up.

"Pork and Pins?" Clark turned away from paying the cabdriver, his expression frozen somewhere between horror and humor.

"You'll love it," she cooed, believing just the opposite. He'd dragged her into his world with the high-stakes business meeting and now it was her turn to introduce him to the world she knew best. "It's just the greatest little twenty-four-hour bowling alley."

"Bowling twenty-four hours a day?" He arched one eyebrow, studying the place without moving forward. "So, the fun never has to stop."

Becky had known he would hate it. She'd selected

it based on its potential to be the most distasteful place on earth to him—the most distasteful place that she would actually go to herself and enjoy, that is. That should teach the man to offer her money in one breath and flirt with her in the next, to tempt her with dreams of a life-style and the hint of romance that could never become an enduring haven for a girl like her. For him, that kind of dalliance cost very little in terms of his wealth or his self-esteem; for her it could well cost the things she held most dear—her self-worth, her determination and her plans for a future based on sound values and permanency.

She plastered on a sweet smile and crinkled her nose. "Fun and good food, too. Pork and Pins has the best barbecued pork sandwiches in town."

"The best, huh?" His eyes twinkled. "Well, I do always enjoy the best."

He strode forward, his hand extended to guide her at his side.

Becky blinked. *Enjoy* it? She'd brought the man here as an object lesson in reality—for her own sake more than his. Now Clark said he intended to enjoy it?

Could she have been so wrong about all this? What if their two worlds could coincide and the two of them were cozily able to move back and forth with ease? She *had* already proven herself in his business world and here he stood ready to give a pork-serving bowling alley a try. Maybe she had misjudged him, and with that, misjudged their chances at exploring a real relationship.

His flattened palm pressed against the small of her back, infusing it with warmth as he ushered her forward. He reached for the door only to have it flung open before them.

All Clark needs to do is wave his hand to have doors open for him, she reminded herself. That's *his* reality, his typical, everyday expectation.

"Welcome to Pork and Pins's Piled Platter Party." A young man's clearly bored face peered out at them from the hole in his once-white plush costume—a giant bowling pin. "Please partake of premium proportions, all you can eat, for one preposterously paltry price."

"Our purpose precisely." Clark never missed a beat, propelling Becky forward past the lethargic greeter as though the scruffy character with his pig's ears poking out from beneath a gold plastic crown was the maître d' of a fine restaurant.

Okay, this wasn't Clark's everyday expectation, she felt sure, but he handled it as though he ran into torpid teens dressed as piggy kingpins on a daily basis. A girl had to be impressed with that, didn't she?

Inside the building, the smells of machine oil and floor wax, nachos and beer mingled with a thin layer of cigarette smoke. Becky waited a moment to let her eyes adjust to the contrast of total darkness and the bright lights of video games and vending machines. Music blared, punctuated by the sounds of a couple of lanes of bowlers knocking down pins.

The piggy-pin person behind them lifted one white gloved hand to point to the end of the long building. "Eats are in there. No food off the carpeted areas. No carryout. No refunds."

"No problem," Becky said, trying to sound as gracious as Clark had, but the teen ignored her entirely.

Clark gave the young man a nod. A nod. That was it.

The teen responded with a grin that hinted he knew something Becky did not and swept out his hand. "Have at it, man."

"We shall, your highness." Clark escorted her inside.

"Your what?"

"Well, he is wearing a crown." The glaring light from the illuminated lanes allowed her to see the fun sparking in Clark's dark eyes. "Does that make him the prince of pork? Or is he wearing that to remind us all that bowling is, after all, the sport of kings?"

"Oh, here it comes," Becky said quietly, preparing herself for the inevitable put-down a man like this would have for her choice of entertainment.

"Here *what* comes?" He made a show of looking around them in a state of alarm. "Is there something more on hand? A wine steward dressed as a little bowling ball, perhaps?"

"Wine steward. That's a good one." Becky laughed without cracking a smile.

Clark laughed in earnest and urged her forward toward the doors with a sign proclaiming the Pork and Pins's sandwiches to be "Bar-B-Licious!"

Why was he being such a good sport about this? She plodded forward. Didn't he realize she'd brought him here to chase him off forever? How would she ever get rid of this man and the lure of dreaming about him as her shining prince if he did not cooperate? She wanted to kick him or stomp on his expensive Italian leather shoes.

Shoes! Becky turned toward the counter where a

barrel-chested man with a stubby cigar was handing out red-and-green rental shoes. "Let's bowl a few frames before we eat—you know, to work up an appetite."

One look at those rental shoes, she figured, and Clark Winstead would give up all pretense of being such a down-to-earth guy and show his true color—money green.

"I thought we came here to eat."

"But it's bowling and barbecue. Don't you want to soak in the full effect?" She folded her arms and waited.

In the distance, someone bowled a strike and began whooping. A few feet away, the man with the cigar tossed a pair of well-worn shoes onto the counter for a customer, coughing on the pathetic footwear as he did.

Clark, with one hand in his pants pocket, pulling his suit jacket back in a pose of pure, relaxed elegance, looked around them. "Well, I've heard of women soaking in mud baths to improve their complexions. How much worse can this be?"

"You mean you're going to stay?"

"Yes, that's exactly what I mean." He looked down into her eyes. Then smiled.

That smile went straight through her, making her knees go liquid and putting a significant chink in the wall she had built to keep any hope for this impossible relationship from taking root. "Gee, you're not at all the kind of snotty rich type I thought you'd be, you know. You're...you're just...you're—"

"Bar-B-Licious?" he offered with a wink.

And then some, she thought. Now more than any

time before, Becky felt entirely unsure where this relationship might be going. But she also felt, for the first time since she laid eyes on this fabulous, powerful man, that her dreams of a relationship with him might someday stand a chance of coming true after all.

Chapter Five

"I can't believe you did the strike dance!" In the dim light of Becky's hallway, Clark waited for her to paw through her purse for her key.

"I don't think you could call it a *dance*, precisely," he said in his defense. "More of a…" He crossed his arms in an X over his chest and gyrated his hips a few times to demonstrate.

Becky broke out in a giggle.

Clark liked the way her whole face lit up when she did that. He liked it enough that he didn't even mind what he had had to do to encourage the response. "Besides, I had it on the best of authority that not doing the strike dance could have dire consequences."

"Gutter balls." She nodded solemnly. "The humiliation."

"I can imagine." He feigned a shudder, hoping for another peal of laughter from her.

"Oh, like you'd have to worry about that." She glared up at him, that laughter almost, but not quite, ready to spill from her lush lips. Her hands stilled in their search inside her purse. She adjusted her leg to better prop up her handbag, which remained precariously balanced on her upraised thigh. "No, sir. No gutter balls for you. Not for Mr. Nearly-Perfect-Game-The-First-Time-Out."

"You can just call me perfect for short," he teased.

She raised her chin, her eyes fixed on his. Her mouth pressed close as if she was actually going to say the word *perfect* but then thought better of it. Instead, she just stood there, hand in her purse, purse on her leg, anticipation on her earnest face.

He wanted to kiss her.

She wet her lips and gave him a look that all but asked him to do just that.

He stepped forward.

She put her leg down and moved toward him.

In a moment, his arms enveloped her, feeling at once the frailty of her slender body and the strength of her quiet passion. Her body pressed close to his, conforming to his hard muscles in all the most intimate places. His lips found hers, and though he tried to hold back the intensity of the longing he'd felt for her almost from their first meeting, he could not rein it all in.

He drew her close, so close he knew she couldn't help but know how much he wanted her, wanted this kiss to go further. He dipped his tongue between her lips, asking, then urging them to part for him.

He didn't want simply to kiss her, to pleasure her and then to draw his own desperate pleasure from her.

He wanted, in that one kiss, in that one moment, to possess her. To lay a claim on her.

That startling revelation made him stop short. He pulled away, blinking as he tried to recover his senses. There were only two ways he could lay claim to Becky—his way or hers.

His way was fun and games and quick, painless goodbyes before anything serious could develop. It was the best of everything money could buy and nothing more emotionally taxing than mutual attraction, genuine affection and the kind of lovemaking that came from those pleasant but insubstantial connections.

Her way involved happily ever afters and marriage vows...and children. *Children.* Something twisted deep in his gut. Suddenly, the image of a little girl with dark curls and Becky's eyes or a son with Becky's spirit and Clark's quiet intensity threatened to overwhelm him.

He stepped back. The realization of how much he liked the idea of having children with this woman caught him completely off guard. He didn't know what to do with that kind of thinking. It didn't fit in with his life plans—and yet...

If he were ever going to have children, he thought he'd found the one person he could trust to be a mother to them. A woman who was not after his money or on a fast track for advancement in his business, though she was smart enough for that she'd already demonstrated. She wanted to make her way on her own. She didn't want anything from him—but the one thing he didn't think he could ever give anyone—himself.

He admired her for all those reasons, including, perhaps most of all, her willingness to take a chance on the deeper kinds of relationships that he, as a man experienced in such things from childhood, knew did not exist. And he *wanted* her for so many more intriguing reasons.

His gaze tripped over her swollen lips. He brushed her warm cheek with his thumb. Yes, he wanted her but just not on her terms. "I'm sorry about that. I had no right to—"

"Don't apologize. If I hadn't wanted you to kiss me, you wouldn't have." Becky looked away before she could have seen the smile he couldn't contain spread over his face at her bravado.

A kitten who thinks her claws make her a tiger. His first impression of her had not been wrong.

Her keys jangled as she finally pulled them free from her purse and began fiddling with them to weed out the worn old brass door key. He thought about reaching out to still the trembling in her hands but decided the gesture would not be welcomed.

"Oh, gosh, I know I can get this...." Her purse strap slid down the length of her slender arm and her purse went plummeting to the floor with a thud.

Across the hallway, the creaking of a door opening just an inch drew Clark's attention. One eye peered out, trained solely on him like a laser beam cutting through the dark to find its mark. He turned to say something reassuring, but before he could begin to speak, the door bumped shut again.

"Looks like we've awakened Mrs. Mendlebaum," he said, turning back to Becky.

"Better than a guard dog." Becky untangled her

arm from the strap, then tried again to sort out the right key in the yellowed light of the old building's dingy hallway. "I guarantee you that if you are still in my apartment at midnight, Mrs. M will be pounding on the door wanting to know if I'm all right."

"She needn't worry." He lifted the clinking key chain from Becky's delicate fingers, then stepped up to fit the proper key into the lock. It made a quiet but decisive click.

"She needn't worry because you'll be gone by midnight?" She tipped her head, her smile tinged with sadness. "Gee, I thought that was Cinderella's modus operandi, not the handsome prince's."

"I assure you, my dear, I have no intention of turning into a pumpkin." He pushed at the stubborn door until it came open. Then he reached inside to flick on a light so he could glance around her quiet, neat apartment. All seemed in order there, so he stepped back to allow her to go in first, his gaze following her every move. "And whether I'm still here at midnight or not…"

She looked back at him over her shoulder in a candid pose that struck him as earthy come hither mixed with wide-eyed innocence—a more potent combination he had never known.

"Whether I'm still here at midnight or not," he continued, his entire body as tight as his voice. "Mrs. M has no reason to worry. As long as you are with me, Becky, you will be all right."

He hadn't meant it as a pledge of honor, but just to let her know he would not press his advantage unless she wanted it pressed. However, once the words were out and he saw the light his promise inspired flickering in the depths of Becky's engaging eyes, he knew he meant them as more than gentlemanly reassurance. Becky called up in him a protective edge, a deeply masculine need to defend her virtue—and to possess it for himself.

Since he would not marry, not anyone, not ever, he knew one desire canceled the other and he knew he had to choose. As he looked into Becky's trusting eyes, the choice was clear to him. "Now that you are safely home, I'd better get going myself."

Even the offer of hot tea and freshly baked cookies could not deter him. Well, had she really thought it would? A man like that? Champagne and caviar were more his style and the kind of women who had those things on hand were his kind of women.

Becky tossed her purse onto the chair by the closet in one swift movement, then turned to shut the front door.

"Psssst."

She jerked her head up in surprise. "Mrs. Mendlebaum?"

"Pssst."

"Yeah, I heard that part, Mrs. Mendlebaum." She stepped to the threshold of her apartment and addressed the sliver of Mrs. Mendlebaum's face peering out from the three-inch opening between her neighbor's door and its frame. "Was there something you wanted to tell me?"

"Psst, Becky. Such a handsome man!"

"Only if you like them tall, gorgeous, rich, witty and...oh, yeah, a good sport, too."

"Ah, he's good at sports, too?"

"No, I meant that he…" Becky raised her voice as she shook her head, then stopped herself. "Actually, yes, he probably is good at sports. I suspect he's good at everything he does."

She touched her fingertip to her lips. Her mouth still tingled from the force of his kiss, from the longing his embrace had ignited in her.

"You're good, too." Mrs. Mendlebaum nodded her head hard enough to rustle the toilet paper wrapped delicately around her head to preserve her bouffant hairdo of silver-blue curls. "A good girl."

"Yippee for me." Becky sighed. "I'm broke, unemployed and haven't had a real date, much less a real…relationship since I moved to Chicago. And I just turned down a chance to be treated to one of the finest restaurants in town—and who knows what else?—or a trip to the bowling alley. No wonder Clark went running out of here at his very first chance. A good girl? Mrs. Mendlebaum? If I had a chance to do it all over again—"

"You'd do exactly the same thing."

Becky gritted her teeth, ready to deny the claim, but she just couldn't do it. She sighed, slumping against the door frame. "Yeah, you're probably right."

"See? A good girl." Mrs. Mendlebaum slapped her hands together. A light flicked on behind her. She huffed and puffed out her ample cheeks, slapped her hands together again and the sound-activated light went out again. "You'll see. Being a good girl, it's not a bad thing. The man—the good sport—he'll be back."

"I don't think so, Mrs. Mendlebaum." Becky

looked down the hallway to the stairwell where Clark had disappeared minutes ago. "A man like that—what would he want with a girl like me anyway?"

"Want?" The question came out in something caught between a squawk and a snort and it left no doubt that Mrs. Mendlebaum thought the question ridiculous. She opened her door a bit wider and leaned out enough to squint her eyes up at Becky, her head nodding slowly. "Young lady, the man wants what all men want."

Becky raised an eyebrow. "You're probably right about that, too, Mrs. M, but a man like Clark hardly needs me to provide him with that. He probably has women lined up around the block ready to give him everything he wants in that regard."

"He wants a wife."

"A wi—I beg your pardon?"

"A wife. Mr. Good Sport wants a wife. A home—and children, too." Mrs. Mendlebaum gestured casually as if her opinion was the world's most common knowledge. "Just like all men."

"Not *this* man. If he did want those things, he'd have them by now. You don't have to know Clark Winstead very long to see that he goes after what he wants and he probably always gets it."

Her neighbor shrugged, causing her faded old housecoat to bunch. "So, maybe he just doesn't know he wants them yet."

"I doubt that. He strikes me as the kind of man who knows exactly what he wants."

"If he doesn't know he wants it yet..." The robustly built neighbor let her voice trail off, then pushed the lapels of her robe closed and cocked her head. "...it's up to you to make him understand what he's missing and then..."

Becky shook her head. "Maybe that's how things were done when you were dating, Mrs. M, but now things are different. Men and women don't play those kinds of games anymore."

"Pffft," Mrs. Mendlebaum commented, batting away the notion with one hand. "Men and women have been playing the same games since Adam and Eve, young lady. Every generation only thinks they have reinvented the rules. Ach, the stories I could tell you about Mr. Mendlebaum when we were courting...such a scoundrel you never saw!"

"Really?" Becky tried to imagine that about the frail-looking little man whom she saw every Tuesday morning taking out the exact same size of neatly wrapped trash.

"He didn't think he wanted to get married, either, but then he met me, and a little nudge here, a little hint there, a few kisses and at least one warning slap on the hands... Forty-six years now we're married, with two gorgeous sons, the older in Iowa and the baby in Cincinnati."

"You slapped Mr. Mendlebaum?" Not only did that news startle her, but Becky wanted desperately to avoid another speech about the Mendlebaums' two perfect, gorgeous, such-a-catch sons, their wives and the to-die-for darling grandkids.

"Of course I slapped him. He deserved it. On the hands only, but still, he learned his lesson. I was a good girl, too, you know." She pulled back her shoulders, her chin—chins—raised with pride.

Becky smiled.

"Chester got over the slapping, but he didn't get over me. I told him it was love—he said it was his liver. I told him his heart was aching for me—he said his heart was burning from my mother's cooking. But that little feeling, that funny little pain inside, right here—" she made a jab in the middle of her lace-armored bosom "—that, he could not run away from. So, before long, he started to run after—after me, of course. And when he finally caught me…ooooh, such passion!"

The very vision of spindly-legged Chester Mendlebaum, with his perpetually bowed back and combed-over hair, in courtship mode made Becky rush to change the subject before she heard anything that might permanently scar her romantic psyche. "This is not the same, though, really it isn't. I was helping Clark with work tonight, that's all. I probably will never see him again—unless it's from a distance sometime when he's getting into a limo with a beautiful woman on his arm."

"Beautiful woman? Limo? Nothing," Mrs. Mendlebaum said. She snapped her fingers, then began to waggle one in Becky's direction. "I'm telling you, that's not what he wants."

Becky rolled her eyes, wondering if her neighbor would understand the subtle sarcasm in her response. "Yeah, sure, right. He wants me."

"You said it," Mrs. Mendlebaum remarked, holding both hands up. "I didn't say it."

"I was just kid—"

"But let me tell you—" she jabbed a finger in Becky's direction "—he wants you. And this man, this good sport, he'll be back."

"B-but I don't think—"

"Pffft. He'll be back. Trust me. He's another Chester Mendlebaum, that one."

It took all of Becky's control not to burst out laughing at the image of Clark dressed in classic Chester wear: checkered pants pulled up to his armpits with an inch of his shins showing between the pants' hem and his sagging black socks.

"No, Mrs. M, I think your Chester is one of a kind." Becky hoped that was diplomatic enough.

"Ach! He's a man. Mr. Good Sport is a man." Mrs. Mendlebaum gave another shrug as she slowly closed the door on her final divination. "He'll be back. You'll see, he will be back."

Don't leave things like this, a little voice nagged in Clark's mind. *You have to go back up there and handle this properly and you have to do it now.* Clark glanced up at the steps he had just descended. He narrowed his eyes as if that might help him better see the right path to follow. All he saw in his mind's eye was Becky standing in that hallway.

He should have asked her, he told himself. He should never have assumed she would reject a relationship, such as he had to offer, on his terms. And now he'd never know—unless he marched back up those stairs and asked.

His footsteps echoed in the cold, dark stairwell. Still, they sounded as sure and hard as his resolve to finish off this matter once and for all. Not knowing what Becky might say to his proposal—his proposition, he corrected for the second time in one night— left a loose thread dangling in an affair he wanted all neatly sewed up with a tidy little knot to guarantee it wouldn't come unraveled again.

He rounded the corner on the last flight of stairs. Becky's voice and that of another woman, one with a muffled accent, carried down to him. He couldn't make out what they were saying, and as he neared the top of the stairs, he heard one door softly fall shut.

"Night, Mrs. Mendlebaum." Becky's raised voice reached him just as he bounded up the last of the steps and moved into the feeble light of the drab hallway.

"Becky, don't go in yet. There's something I have to ask you."

She glanced from her open door to him, then at the door across the way, then to him again. Her eyes took on a deer-in-the-headlight quality for only a moment before she paused, sighed, then cocked her head and smiled. "So, there *is* a little bit of Chester in you after all."

He tucked one hand in his pants pocket, letting his jacket do a bit of a casual slouch as he, too, tipped his head and smiled at the peculiar and yet intriguing response. "I beg your pardon?"

She started to point to the door on the other side of the hall, then curled her finger in and shook her head. Lifting her shoulders up in a way that made her seem like a little girl with a hand caught in the cookie jar, she shook her head. "Never mind."

He nodded.

She nodded.

He tripped his gaze over her, drinking her in. She looked wonderful to him. Even more lovely and vital than she had looked fifteen minutes ago when he'd first delivered her to her apartment door. But then fifteen minutes ago he had not yet tasted those sweet lips. Fifteen minutes ago he had not come up with the plan to keep her in his life, yet keep his life on the same steady course he had always preferred. Just the hope that she might say yes to him, that she might consent to the kind of arrangement he had in mind for them, cast everything in a warmer light than before.

"You said you came back to ask me something?" She took a step toward him.

"Yes. Yes, I did." He stayed put. Let her come to him, he thought. Always let your opponent come to you. That was smart business and, let's face it, he told himself, this was going to be pure business at its heart.

He ignored the nagging irony that he had, in fact, come to her. He had just placed himself in a position to make it easier for her to make the move, he told himself, ignoring, too, the transparent ego-massaging of that thought. Just as he ignored that niggling pain right beneath his breastbone that some might call his conscience or some telltale emotion welling up, trying to break free from behind his long-walled-off heart.

All he had to say to that was…pork. That's all it was—greasy, barbecued pork from the night's fare playing havoc with his digestive system.

"Clark?"

"Hmm?"

"Your question?"

She stood close enough for him to see the light in the depths of her eyes, smell the suddenly evocative mix of her simple shampoo and the distinct odor of

Pork and Pins. "Do you know how wonderful you smell tonight?"

"*That's* your question?" Disappointment flickered in those gorgeous eyes.

He smiled and reached out to put one hand under her chin. His gaze sank into hers. "My question is, Becky, that is, I'm wondering if you would be interested in…if I could possibly convince you to—"

"Yes." Her answer cut short his rambling and his searching for the most delicate way to present his idea.

"But you don't even know what I'm going to ask."

"I don't have to know, Clark." She lifted her shoulders, her hands behind her back and her head high. The yellow light gleamed in the masses of her golden curls and made her luminous eyes glitter. "You promised me that whenever I was with you I'd always be all right."

"I did, didn't I?"

"And I believed you."

"You would," he muttered, angry only at himself and that damned moment of nobility.

"I beg your pardon?"

"You've got that all turned around. It's me who should be begging—for your forgiveness, Becky. I never should have—"

"Whatever it is, it's forgotten now." She whisked her hand through the air. "You came back, Clark. That's what matters. Now, what is it you wanted to ask me to do?"

"To tie a knot in a thread," he said, knowing she'd have no idea what that actually meant to him. He crossed his arms, feeling like a damned fool for not having gotten out when the getting was good.

"To tie…a knot…? Clark, are you saying—"

"I'd like you to go away with me, Becky. On a short trip, maybe over a long weekend." Compromise. He didn't like it, but it was a valid tool in any transaction, especially one between the sexes. If he could get her away, arrange some private time, he could present his idea to her slowly. A nice trip to the right locale could allow him to gradually expose her to the fact that many other options awaited them besides the till-death-us-do-part route. "While we're there, I'd like us to spend time getting to know one another, separate bedrooms and all, of course. That is, until we—"

"Yes!" She threw her arms around him and began showering his cheeks with kisses.

"Good. It's settled then." With her kissing him, he felt anything but settled. He stepped back. He hadn't gotten what he had come for, but he had gotten as good as he could expect, he reasoned.

Becky put her hand in his. "Maybe now you'll come inside for those cookies and…whatever."

He watched her lips with baited intensity as they formed her last word with an enticing breathy quality.

"I…uh…I…" He placed his hand over the deepening pain in his chest. "I don't think I should. We'll have plenty of time together later. For now, I have a lot of arrangements to make."

"Oh, of course. Me, too." She gave his hand a squeeze as if they shared some tender secret.

He tried to squeeze her hand back, but that weird little ache, like nothing he'd known before, drew most of his strength. He sighed, then stepped away from her again. ''I'll call you tomorrow to give you the details.''

"Okay. I'll be waiting."

If he had any sense at all, he'd *leave* her waiting, Clark thought as he headed back down the stairs. But he wouldn't leave her waiting. He couldn't any more than she could probably live her life waiting for him to do the one thing he'd had no intention of ever doing—getting married.

Chapter Six

"Put these in your purse. You're going to need them."

Becky looked up from the half-packed suitcase lying open on her bed to stare at the plain brown bag Mrs. Mendlebaum had thrust toward her. "Can I ask what *they* are or is it a surprise?"

"Just a little something you are going to need. Trust me." She gave the bag, pinched closed at the top by her thumb and forefinger, a shake. "As soon as you told me about this...this...this...trip you are taking with the handsome man who is good at everything, I told my Chester I had to go down to the drugstore and get these for you."

"Oh? You did?" Becky recoiled only slightly. Now she understood what *they* were, of course. She smoothed her palm down the protective plastic bag covering her simple sheath party dress. And while she did not want to appear ungrateful or unsophisticated about it, she couldn't help but feel uneasy over the obviously well-intentioned gesture. "Maybe you should put...them on the dresser and I'll see to them later."

"No, I want you should look *now*." The rattle of the bulging paper bag underscored her insistence. "I got all kinds, everything they had, and you should see how much they had!"

Becky choked back a gasp. Acts of concerned kindness aside, Becky hardly thought the plump little old blue-haired lady from across the hall should be buying her...providing her with...

"All natural, extrastrength, long lasting. Ach, who knew people needed all these choices?"

"Um, uh, that was sure nice of you to think of me...that way." Becky cringed and busied herself even more frantically with her packing. In truth, she wished her thoughtful, nosy, elderly neighbor would not think of her that way at all—as the kind of girl who would be needing a paper bag filled with...and especially not the extrastrength, long lasting kind.

"Here, your hands are full. I'll show you."

"Mrs. Mendlebaum, no!" She reached her hands out beneath the upturned bag as though she could stop the outpouring of what she expected to be every kind of condom imaginable into her suitcase. "Please leave them in the bag. I don't want to risk having one fall into one of my pockets and my not knowing it, then putting on an outfit and have Clark see that I've come on this trip loaded down with...antacids?"

"Keep a few in your purse at all times. For the pain." She pounded her fist to her impressive chest.

"The pain?"

"The one he's going to say is indigestion, but we know better. We know it's true love."

"You're telling me that the man I'm going away with to get to know before we tie the knot can't tell true love from tainted leftovers?" Becky laughed and shook her head.

"Men!" Mrs. Mendlebaum rolled her eyes. "What do they know about love? It's our duty as women to lead them into it, gently but without taking any of their nonsense."

Becky laughed and turned to grab up the last of her things for packing. "I keep telling you, Mrs. Mendlebaum, things aren't like that now. Things are far more direct and uncomplicated."

"Love uncomplicated?" She snorted. "Where's the fun in that?"

"I'm sure it's still quite fun. It's just not the same as in your day," Becky assured her.

"No, it's not." Mrs. Mendlebaum lumbered over to the doorway, then turned for a parting shot. "In my day, young lady, the man and the woman waited until *after* the wedding to go away together."

"Goodbye, Mrs. M, and thank you for the thoughtful gift." Becky flashed a smile she hoped would convey her good humor and also cover up her own misgivings about the nature of the trip with Clark as she watched the meddling neighbor let herself out.

When Mrs. Mendlebaum had shut the door soundly behind her, Becky let out a sigh. Of course, she would have preferred things to have gone in the old-fashioned order, wedding then going away together. But she really didn't know Clark well enough to vow forever after with him, did she? This trip would give them both the chance to get to know one another and then...

She laid down the last two garments she'd selected to bring along—two distinctly different choices in nightclothes. She patted her trusty old Woodbridge High size XXL T-shirt, the one Frankie McWurter had loaned her and she'd never given back. That's what she slept in most of the time. Just touching the thin gray jersey with the faded orange-red letters on it made her think of home and all the wholesome, ordinary things that made up life back there.

Then she trailed her fingertips over the silky slip of lace edged fabric on the gown she'd bought with her last bit of extra cash from her temp perfume job. It wasn't too elegant, she knew, but then, she imagined it would not have to be because if she had occasion to wear it, the gown would not stay on her body very long.

The thought of Clark's large, strong hands on that flimsy fabric with her own skin just beneath made her cheeks warm and her heart pound. She had no idea if this trip would actually end in a honeymoon as she hoped, but she certainly wanted to be prepared if it did.

On that thought, she thumped the suitcase closed, snapped the locks down tight and snatched up the handle. Spinning on her heel, she readied herself to go downstairs and wait for Clark's car. She took a step, then two, then pivoted again.

In a moment of something between superstition and high anxiety, she grabbed up a handful of the stomach remedies Mrs. Mendlebaum had provided, tucked them in her purse, then raised her chin high and marched toward the door and whatever destiny lay beyond it.

"She should be here in a few minutes, Baxter." Clark maneuvered his body so that he could keep one eye on the leaded glass door of Rosemont House, a quaint little bed-and-breakfast nestled in rural Indiana.

His gaze moved from the rich, gleaming wood of the entryway to the L-shaped stairway of the immaculate old Victorian home. His secretary had chosen well and he made a mental note to reward her with a bonus. He glanced out the window at the flower-lined walk, the pristine porch swing, the perfection of the spring afternoon. He corrected that mental note—a bonus and a long weekend off. Rosemont House was the perfect place for him to have a frank, open conversation with Becky regarding future…interactions between them, without the frantic distractions of his usual haunts. No nightclubs or casinos, no business or social obligations to take his mind off his goal. No fancy clothes, overly made-up faces or false friendships to take away from the real reason he had whisked Becky away from Chicago for the weekend.

Here, in this serene setting, where nobody knew either of them, he could calmly and rationally lay out the plan he'd formulated over these past few days. That plan—to offer Becky a position in his company and a place in his bed, both with clearly defined legal protections for both of them—was as far as he would go toward anything that even resembled marriage.

He doubted that she would accept it, but he had to put forth the offer and hear the answer that would either move them forward or end their relationship forever. Either way, the whole business of Becky Taylor would be done with and he could get on with his life instead of dwelling on the wickedly wonderful imagined possibilities with the woman.

"Clark? Clark, old buddy, you there?"

Clark cleared his throat, brought suddenly back to reality by his friend's voice on the phone. "Yes, I was just…looking out the front window for the car. They should arrive shortly."

"I still don't get why you didn't drive up there together." Suspicion colored Baxter's voice.

"You know I've been in New York on business. It just seemed simpler to fly into Indianapolis from there, then rent a car and drive here myself while my driver brought her."

"How is that simpler than you flying back to Chicago and driving over with her?"

His old friend had a point, but Clark didn't want to admit it, least of all to Baxter. Ever since he'd met this young woman, he had hardly been able to think straight and he didn't like that, didn't like it one bit. He had hoped the time alone driving through the Indiana countryside would clear his head, steel his nerves, quiet his libido.

Clark gripped the phone in his hand and leaned back against the oversize check-in desk that dominated the foyer of Rosemont House. He narrowed his eyes on the undisturbed front drive and the small gravel parking lot bathed in sparkling sunlight, knowing the car bringing Becky to him would soon be there.

Besides, when ready to clinch a deal, you always make the other person come to you. Becky was making this trip of her own volition, and in doing so, admitting that she wanted him as much as he wanted her. And he did want her. The thought of just how badly he wanted her made his body tighten.

He'd done the right thing in coming ahead alone. Four hours in the back seat of a car with Becky and who knew what might happen? His mind threatened to supply him with some enticing examples when Baxter's voice interceded instead.

"I mean, my friend, you set a girl up for a Winstead conquest, the least you can do is give the sacrificial virgin a lift up the mountain before you plant your flag on her but good."

"Winstead conquest? Sacrificial virg…" Clark gritted his teeth, his pulse suddenly pounding in his temples, heat rising from beneath his crisp white collar. He'd extended an offer and she had come of her own choosing; while that did say something about Clark's personal power in the matter, it hardly spoke of conquest and sacrifice. "You don't know what the hell you're talking about, Baxter. But I will tell you this. If you ever, even in jest, *ever* use a crude sexual innuendo like 'plant your flag' regarding Rebecca Taylor again, I'll—"

"Hey, hey, pal. Calm down. You're the one who's putting a sexual take on that remark. I was just referring back to a conversation we had about why you're never going to get married."

Clark blinked. His mind paged back through the days. He did remember such a conversation, when Baxter had told him that he would never marry because he would always feel anyone he became involved with would be beholden to him. "Yes, I'm sorry. I do recall that conversation. I didn't agree with it then and I don't agree with it now.''

"Uh-huh." Baxter's tone implied, "Tell me another whopper." Then he chuckled before saying, "Then tell me why it is, in all the years I've known you, I've never seen you go this overboard over any woman—until you met one who wouldn't take your money, wouldn't even let you buy her an elegant meal and evening on the town? The kind of girl who is going to be more content alone with you in the middle of Indiana than rubbing elbows with the rich and famous on the French Riviera?"

Clark started to give his friend a perfectly reasonable explanation for his behavior, having to do with needing to tie up loose ends and finding a mutually satisfying resolution to some basic human attractions and urges. He started to—but just then Becky's car turned into the drive and his mind went blank save for thoughts of seeing her again.

"Clark?"

"Hmmm?" The sleek black car pulled to a stop, creating a small cloud of gray dust. Moments later, a large red vehicle rolled into the parking spot beside it. Looks like they'd have to share the bed-and-breakfast with other guests, Clark thought. Not that he cared. No one else would intrude on his much awaited time with Becky. No one else would have an effect on the things he had to ask her or the plans he wanted to present to her. Clark dismissed the red vehicle and the family piling out of it to focus solely on the dark car and its one very special passenger.

"Clark, are you listening?" Baxter's voice seemed tinny and far away.

"Mmm." In a flash, the driver leaped out and had the rear door open. Becky's shapely legs slid from inside the car. She planted her feet firmly, then drew herself up to her full height. Sunlight glinted off her hair and created a tantalizing play of light and shadow over the curves of her body. Clark felt a slow, appreciative smile ease over his lips. "Listen, Baxter, I have to go. She's here."

"Sheesh, Clark, guess I owe you an apology."

Clark, who had started to put the phone down, raised it to his ear again. "What was that? What do you have to apologize to me for?"

"That crack about this new woman being your latest conquest. If I'd only known—"

"Known what?"

"That this lady didn't come all that way to throw herself on your romantic mercy, pal. She came to claim what's already hers. At long last, the conqueror has been conquered!"

Clark started to protest the ridiculous assessment, but Baxter had already hung up. He snorted and dropped the receiver in its cradle. Becky had come to him because it was convenient for both of them and because when you want to make a deal with someone, you let them come to you. It gives you the upper hand.

He heard the door swing open. Becky's soft-soled shoes scuffed lightly over the hardwood floor. Clark adjusted his tie, tucked one hand in his pocket, then smiled with measured nonchalance, prepared to charm the pants—figuratively if not literally—off the young woman he'd asked to meet him here.

He chuckled to himself as he turned with calculated

casualness. The conqueror had been conquered? What
a load of—

"Baby smooches!" Becky spun around in the
doorway just in time to intercept two children who
had obviously crawled out of that gargantuan red jelly
bean of a vehicle that had pulled up alongside Clark's
car.

The two fair-haired tots actually threw themselves
into Becky's open arms in a peal of giggles and loud,
smacking kisses. Even in his confusion over the incident, Clark had to admit the sight had an appeal all
its own. It warmed and amused him, and he'd have
told Becky as much if that odd pain in the middle of
his chest hadn't picked just that time to flare up.

He pressed two fingers to his breastbone and
winced.

Just then, a smiling, attractive couple breezed in
through the doorway arm in arm. Becky stood, ex-
changed embraces with each adult, then grabbed the
tiny hands of the two children at her sides and swirled
around, creating a picture so glowing with wholesome
happiness that Norman Rockwell couldn't have added
any finer touches to it.

"I hope you don't mind, Clark." Becky glanced
back at the tall, muscular man standing behind her,
then at the lovely dark-haired woman wrapped in the
mantle of his arm. "But since this trip is so close to
my hometown, I thought it might be a good time for
you to meet my family."

The conqueror, Clark thought as he tried to make
his mind grasp that bizarre twist in his well-laid plans,
had just been totally confounded.

* * *

"When I called my brother to tell him we'd be staying at Rosemont House this weekend, I never imagined he'd take it upon himself to show up at the exact same time I did." Becky glanced up from the hand-drawn map Mr. Rose, the owner of the bed-and-breakfast, had provided, to study Clark's chiseled profile. A fine profile. Classic. Made more angular and masculine by the underlying tension in the set of his jaw. Less than an hour into their getting-to-know-one-another trip and things had already gone awry. Ah, well, it would make a great story to tell their grandkids, she thought, trying to cheer herself. Cocking her head in what she pictured as an adorable mix of whimsy and resignation, she grinned. "According to the map, the picnic pavilion is just around this bend."

Clark nodded, guiding the car he had taken to the bed-and-breakfast expertly along the dusty, narrow road. "What I don't understand is how your brother got here at all. I have to say what an amazing coincidence I find it that my secretary would book us into a discreet little hideaway that just happens to be only an hour's drive from your hometown."

"An hour and a half and there wasn't any coincidence about it. Your secretary called me to say you wanted to book some place where I would feel comfortable. So naturally I started thinking of places close to home that I knew would fit the bill—"

"There goes that bonus," he muttered.

"What?"

"Never mind. Go on. You were saying that you started thinking…"

"Well, maybe it isn't the most sophisticated thing to admit, Clark, but it did occur to me that if I was going to go off with a man I really didn't know all that well, that I'd be wise to keep things on my own turf, as it were.''

"Forget sophisticated. That was smart. The kind of thing I might have done." Admiration colored his tone. "If I'd been offered the same opportunity."

"You set the rules, Clark. It's not my fault you forgot to make them to your own advantage." She laughed, then pointed to an even narrower road that led to a covered area with a picnic table and permanent grill standing at lopsided attention next to it. "Besides, you don't have to worry too much. Matt and Dani are only going to stay for lunch, then head back home."

"That's a long drive for a baloney sandwich," Clark said as the car rocked to a bumpy stop.

"The only baloney my brother cares about is whether or not you're full of it." Becky wiggled her eyebrows at the man, hoping to lighten the mood.

Things weren't off to a roaring start, granted, but it wasn't a total disaster. She had wanted Clark to meet her family and vice versa. So it happened a little out of the planned sequence. Becky knew she could overcome the awkwardness of it and so could Clark if he really wanted to. That was one thing they had in common; they both understood that to get to the goal, one often had to put aside life's inconveniences and do what had to be done.

Clark had proved that time and again, from bringing her the charm he'd had fixed to sealing the deal with the perfume magnate. Her would-be prince wouldn't let uninvited relatives stand in the way of their time to get to know one another to see if they were ready for marriage. Besides, this gave her a chance to show off her maternal instincts while interacting with her niece and nephew.

"Don't worry too much about what Matt might think of you, Clark. He's already entrusted you with his most precious possessions." Becky unlatched her seat belt, then turned to peer back at four-year-old Kyle and his almost-three-year-old sister, Maggie. Her heart swelled with pride and love and something new she had never experienced when gazing at the children she adored—a sense of longing and anticipation.

Clark twisted so that, he, too, could look at the young children in their toddler seats.

The sudden awareness of his being so close only heightened these feelings for Becky. One day would they be driving to a picnic with their own children in the back seat? The possibility thrilled and unnerved her at the same time.

"Don't get me wrong. I'm not complaining, but I have to tell you, I have no idea what to do with children this age. Or any age for that matter." Clark shifted his gaze from the children to Becky and back again. "Do they…speak English?"

His ignorance brought her out of the sappy emotional mood she'd fallen into. She laughed. "Of course they speak English. What language did you think they'd speak?"

"I mean, do they…can they…if I were to say something to you, would they understand it?" Clark eyed Kyle as if he thought the child might suddenly explode or something.

"That would depend on what it is."

"Then to be on the safe side, this had better wait until their parents get here with the food and you and I can go for a walk and grab a few minutes alone."

"Goodness, that sounds important."

"Just a little something I wanted to give you at the beginning of the weekend."

Becky's pulse did a little hopscotch when he reached into his pocket and began to withdraw a small black box like the one that had come from the jeweler who had repaired her charm.

He leaned toward her, his voice nothing more than a rasping whisper. "It's a token, really. A token of how I...of my..."

"Yes?" In forming the words, their lips parted.

Before she could think, Clark's mouth took hers with a hunger she thought only she had known. His tongue caressed her lower lip as though he might try to satisfy that hunger at this very moment. He moved closer and the movement sent a gentle shock wave through her hips and thighs.

Becky dug her fingers into the hard muscles of his arm and neck. She had dreamed of the moment she'd be this close to Clark again since she'd last watched him walk away from her apartment. She edged closer. The kiss broke just long enough for her to murmur, "This is the only token I need now, Clark."

"But I wanted to give you more. So much more." He dropped a kiss on the corner of her mouth, on her cheek, on her temple, then whispered against her lips again, "I want to give—"

She mewed and pressed her body close to his, aware of nothing else but him.

"I wanted to..." His blunt fingers snagged in her hair.

"What?" She searched his eyes. "You want what?"

"I want..." He drew her to him. "I want you."

"Me, too!"

"I want a kiss, too, Aunt Becky!"

The small voices from the back seat ripped away any vestige of romance from the moment.

"Kyle and Maggie." She winced, shutting her eyes only long enough to make the transition from wanting to throw herself at Clark to needing to care for her niece and nephew.

"Kiss me, too, Aunt Becky," four-year-old Kyle demanded again.

"Kiss me! Kiss me!" Maggie squealed.

"They understood *that* pretty well, it seems." Clark eyed her, disappointment shining in his eyes.

But disappointment about what? Becky had to wonder. Disappointment that he couldn't give her whatever token he'd planned? Or that their kiss had been so abruptly interrupted? Or was it something more than that?

Becky thought back to her plan to allow her interaction with the children to show herself to Clark as perfect mother material. Perfect, yeah, right. She'd blown that the minute she'd put her own pleasure before her concern for the kids. And while this incident rated a mere tremor on the miserable-mommy Richter scale, Becky began wondering if her own actions accounted for the disappointment she saw registered in Clark's eyes.

Well, if that was the case, she could not let it happen again. She would show him she was a responsible, caring auntie who could carry those attributes over to her own children tenfold. She'd already shown herself to him as a sharp business negotiator, an eager would-be lover and one heck of a decent bowler. Before the afternoon was over, Clark Winstead would never doubt that she would become anything but the world's greatest mom.

Chapter Seven

"That won't stain." Becky dabbed her paper napkin at the gooey yellow blob of potato salad sliding slowly down the front of Clark's favorite polo shirt.

Across from them, Becky's brother caught up the child responsible for the fledgling food fight. "Margaret Rebecca Taylor, I ought to…"

In the background, the words of Matt Taylor's eye-to-eye brand of heart-to-heart talk blurred with the sound of casual family chaos unleashed by his daughter's actions.

"Mommy, Aunt Becky said no dessert unless we cleaned our plates. Does Maggie throwing her food count?" The young boy called Kyle bounced on the very edge of the attached picnic bench, jostling the table as though it were on springs.

His mother dove to spare the soft-drink cans from tipping over, anchoring them in place with splayed fingers. The pretty woman, with her dark hair caught up in a neat ponytail, never missed a beat or mussed her clothes as she presided over the remains of the meal with a swiftness and competence obviously born of much practice. "No, that does not count, Kyle. Sit still, please, honey, or the drinks will spill."

"You know better than to pull a stunt like that, young lady." Matt's voice overlapped his wife's.

The plastic table covering flapped in the breeze.

Becky sucked in her breath.

"But, Mo-om, her plate *is* clean now! Can't we—"

"That is not how we do things in this family, Miss Maggie," Matt said sternly but without any hurtful anger. "And you know it. Now apologize to Aunt Becky and Mr. Winstead."

Maggie thrust her lower lip out in a move that Clark calculated had wrapped her father around her pinkie more than once. But Matt did not back down. The pair sat glowering at one another. Neither seemed willing to budge on the matter.

"Maggie!" Dani's tone held a weighted warning. "What kind of an impression are we going to leave with Mr. Winstead?"

Clark started to protest that they had not left any kind of impression at all, but of course, they had. He glanced from the barely contained squirminess of Kyle to the frustrated faces of Matt and Dani, to the determined scowl of little Maggie. They'd made an impression all right—or rather they'd confirmed for him an impression he'd formed long ago in his own childhood.

Marriage was mayhem and adding children to the mix only made it more so. He shut his eyes for a moment, thanking heaven for his early insight into this common human blunder. The lesson had come at quite a cost—the nurturing and sense of security he'd lacked as a young boy—but it had served him well. It had kept him from this kind of frantic, doomed life-style. It had helped him find more creative solutions in establishing romantic relationships and perhaps, someday, even procuring progeny.

That thought led him instantly back to Becky. He opened his eyes to find her still fretting over his ru-ined shirt. He drew in the scent of her hair and let himself revel in the warmth of her body just inches from his.

"See, it's coming off—sort of." Becky began to swipe more vehemently until it became a brisk scrub-bing motion that seemed to Clark to be grinding the wet, sticky mess even more thoroughly into his white-and-blue shirt. "What's left will come out with just a little elbow grease and some presoak. Right, Dani?"

"Weelll…" Dani bit into her lower lip, her gaze moving from the glob of food, which her younger child had sent flying, to the label on the grocery store side-dish container. "It does have mustard in it, which is famous for making stains, you know. And then mayo—which is pretty oily—and, let's see, syn-thetic egg yolks with artificial coloring added, pickle relish with yellow dye number 5 and blue dye number 1. Then the preservatives and chemicals—"

"Never mind, Becky." Clark plucked her hand away from his chest, keeping a firm but gentle grasp of her fingers to make sure she didn't suddenly start mashing the mess into his shirt again. "It sounds like something I'd rather be wearing than eating anyway."

He meant it as a joke, but the sudden downward

cast of Becky's usually bright eyes and the almost imperceptible tremble of her lower lip made him feel like a first-class heel.

"I'm sorry." She bowed her head, and the afternoon sunlight bounced off her golden curls and highlighted the sensual curve of her neck. "I've just made a fiasco out of this whole day."

Clark wanted to kiss that neck, but with her brother's keen and watchful eye on them as it had been during the entire picnic, he didn't dare. Instead, he cupped his palm over the place where her neck and shoulder met. "No," he said quietly, "you haven't turned anything into a fiasco."

She turned her cheek toward his hand, her eyes on him.

"You couldn't," he found himself stumbling on, speaking out of a need to comfort and reassure her. He still harbored great hopes for what they could have together. Until he heard otherwise from her, he would not assume that they couldn't find the answer to their longings in one another without the curse of commitment. "In fact, your just being around saves things from becoming a fiasco for me."

"Really?" She lifted just her hesitant gaze to his.

"Really." To Clark's surprise, he meant that in all sincerity, not just as a means of easing the momentary awkwardness. At some point between inadvertently stomping on Becky's sterling charm and having her niece shower him with chemically enhanced potato salad, Clark had stopped thinking of her as the cause of consternation and instead saw her as delivery from it.

"Thank you for saying that," she murmured.

"I meant it." He nodded, unable to get out another word. A quick, sharp pain in his stomach seemed to close off his airway. Clark took a deep breath. At least he thought it was his stomach. It felt higher than that and altogether different from any heartburn or belly-ache he'd ever encountered, but still...

He stole a glance over the aftereffects of their pic-nic fare. Empty chip bags, soda-pop cans, paper nap-kins with greasy fingerprint smears and the telltale pile of chicken bones met his survey, not to mention the suspicious slimy potato salad plastered to his chest. It was his stomach, he concluded without fur-ther speculation. Had to be.

"Well, Maggie, I thought you were a big girl, but I can see now that I was wrong about you." Matt Taylor shook his head, leaned back as much as the bench would allow without tipping them all over and crossed his arms over his chest.

"I am a big girl," Maggie protested.

"How can that be?" Matt twisted his head to the side and looked up at the sky as if pondering a great puzzle. "Big girls don't throw food—and if they do make a mistake like that, they always say they are sorry for what they've done."

Clark smiled at the psychology Matt employed. Still, he pressed two fingers into his solar plexus, hop-ing to counteract the effects of whatever food had gotten inside him, not on his shirt.

"You okay?" Becky whispered.

"Indigestion."

"Oh? Really?" She said it with an element of dis-belief.

"Yes, indigestion." Surely she could tell from his

snarled reply that he wasn't kidding around, he thought, though that hardly justified his surliness.

"Wow." Disbelief seemed to have turned to hushed awe in her tone. "I mean, I *had* hoped. But I never thought—"

"What?" He turned to her. She beamed at him. Beamed. Like a bride in a sappy wedding photo, he thought. Well, she might as well put the dimmer on that expression, Clark decided, because it wasn't going to happen, not for them, not in that way. "Becky, I think we—"

"Here, I have something for your stomach." She leaned down, grabbed up her purse and fished out a pink tablet wrapped in crinkling cellophane.

"Huh?" He tried to make his thoughts and her actions gel into something logical. Who got this happy over offering someone an antacid anyway?

"Here, just take it, and if it doesn't do the trick, I have another kind. In fact, I have a whole bunch of brands right at my fingertips." She said it as if she was talking about something wondrous, miraculous, something she had been searching for all her life.

He took the tablet and just held it between his thumb and forefinger.

"I *am* a big girl." Maggie kicked her foot against the side of the booster chair her parents had brought along. "I am."

"Then you know what you have to do." Matt urged his daughter with a nod of his head in Clark's direction.

The child held her breath in her plump, puffed-up cheeks. Clearly, she did not want to apologize to a total stranger and, just as clearly, her father's designs left her no other acceptable option.

It was a classic business device, but Clark had rarely seen it done with such sweetly subtle maneuvering—except by Matt's baby sister, who was sitting right next to him. Suddenly, he studied the pink tablet caught between his fingers as though it might contain pure hemlock.

"Mr. Wins'ead?" The tiny voice commanded his attention.

"Um, yes? Yes..." He looked into those huge, unassuming eyes, so like her aunt's, and any concerns about Becky melted away. How could anyone with a niece this charming and a family this decent be plotting some kind of romantic coup against his well-laid plans? "Yes, Maggie?"

"M'sorry that I frowed the food and it hitted you and got your shirt all messy." She wriggled her toes in bright yellow sandals and twisted her fat little fingers together over her polka-dotted sundress.

"That's all right." He smiled, then popped the antacid out of its package and lifted it in a kind of salute toward Becky as he said, "I know you weren't actually using me for target practice."

A lightness came over the child at his reaction. Then what seemed a moment of real regret showed in her expression. "I hope your mommy won't be mad at you for getting dirty."

He laughed and gave the child a sly wink. "I think it'll be okay. My mommy isn't even in the country right now."

Matt and Dani laughed.

He poked the pink pill into his mouth, feeling quite pleased with himself.

"You mean you doesn't has a mommy right now?" The child cocked her head and a stray curl flicked against her rosy cheek.

"Every family should have a mommy." Kyle peered at Clark, seeming quite earnestly concerned at his motherless state.

"At this age they tend to think of all adults as either mommies or daddies," Dani explained almost apologetically. "I think what Maggie really means is...well, you know that she thinks everyone should have a...partner. For every daddy, that is, every man, there should be a mommy—in other words, the perfect woman."

"We has a mommy," Maggie said, pointing to her mother. "You need to get one, too."

"Yes, well, I..." he tried to answer around the pill lying on his tongue.

"I know!" The little girl clapped her hands together. "Aunt Becky can be your mommy!"

"Yeah!" Kyle's eyes shone with excitement rivaled only by the flicker of amusement in his parents' faces.

Clark bit down on the tablet Becky had given him. A bitter, chalky taste filled his mouth, keeping him from giving an answer. Which might have been for the best, he thought, given he had no idea what to say to that.

Becky, however, did not seem to have any trouble coming up with a response. "Well, I wouldn't be Clark's mommy, of course, but I hope I'm not spoiling anything when I tell you all not to be too surprised if you hear very soon that this less-than-perfect woman has found her Mr. Right.''

Mr. Who? Him? Clark gulped down the last of the tablet, hoping to speak up and set the matter straight before too much damage was done.

Too late. Dani had already run around the table to throw her arms around Becky in a big hug, and Matt had thrust his huge hand toward Clark in a gesture of congratulations.

"Welcome to the family, Clark, old man. Wasn't sure about all this when Becky first mentioned you. But now, seeing the way you look at my sister and knowing you can certainly provide for her and any family you have together, I give my blessing. I think you two are going to have a great marriage.''

"Live together?" Becky blinked once, then twice, hoping that the next time she opened her eyes she'd find Clark breaking into a big ol' *gotcha* grin.

His face remained as calm and seemingly unemotional as the moment the astonishing words had left his mouth.

Around them, the quiet grounds of Rosemont House provided an atmosphere of domestic tranquillity: lush, manicured greenery, a large, lovely older house with neat white trim, swaying yellow flowers lining the walk. Birds chirped and the breeze made the leaves rustle just enough to make one think of napping in a hammock or idling away the afternoon in the arms of your loved one. That's what Becky had envisioned they'd do after Matt and Dani had gone home and she and Clark had come back to the bed-and-breakfast to clean up, then "talk.''

Clark had said nothing during the ride back to indicate what he wanted to talk about. In fact, he hardly said a word. He just grimaced over his upset stomach and made understanding noises about how nice her family was, how cute the children were, how lovely the scenery was and that kind of thing.

When he had come to her door in a fresh shirt and his hand in his pocket, guarding the token he'd alluded to earlier, she assumed, Becky had expected...

Well, she wasn't sure what she'd expected. Despite the fact that everything about her relationship with Clark had taken on its own whirlwind pace, an engagement did seem too much too soon. But when she had seen the jewelry box he'd wanted to give her, the token of how he felt, she had to wonder.

Reason prevailed, though, and Becky had spent most of the time between getting back to her room and hearing Clark's knock on her door talking herself out of any ideas of marriage and weddings. With her inherited tendency toward reaching for impossible dreams like her father, she feared she might waste too much of her life and livelihood doing just that. Becky had forced herself not to imagine the most wonderful of possibilities regarding Clark.

While she had steeled herself against any illusions that her prince had come with glass slipper—or engagement ring—in hand, nothing could have prepared her for what Clark had actually wanted to present to her. A deal. An arrangement. "A mutually gratifying solution to our physical and emotional needs at the present," as he had so succinctly put it.

"You're saying that you think we ought to live together?" She put her hand to her throat, battling the tightness in her chest. The quick, fluttering movement made the pristine white porch swing where they sat rocking gently.

"Not live together in the usual sense of the term." He spoke with the detachment of a boss correcting his secretary's dictation. "We wouldn't share a home. I don't think that's wise, really, and it defeats the purpose of having a sensible, reciprocally satisfying arrangement such as I'm propo...um, offering."

"Uh-huh. I see." She didn't really see. In fact, their surroundings had dimmed to nothing more than color, light and shadow. Her pulse pounded in her ears and she tried to swallow. Clark's face, even her own hands, became a blur beyond the hot tears that sprang to her eyes.

What a fool she had been. What an absolute, blinded by her own emotions, idiot!

And she had no one to blame but herself. Clark had never broached the subject of marriage. No, that had happened only in her mind, in her dreams. She'd connected the deeper levels of this relationship out of fairy tales and heartsick hopes for something more than Clark had ever wanted or would ever give a girl like her.

If she were Cinderella, as she'd so often thought of herself lately this past week, then the clock had just struck twelve. The fantasy had just evaporated leaving nothing but rags and reality in its wake.

Becky cleared her throat but could not clear away the unshed tears pooling over her vision. She inhaled deeply, Clark's spicy aftershave stinging in her nostrils. She pushed back a frayed curl of hair that had wriggled loose from the silk bow tied on the braid at the back of her neck.

"Are you all right, Becky?" Clark's deep voice vibrated with hushed sincerity.

Perhaps he really did care more than it seemed. Or perhaps she had lost the ability to even tell the difference anymore. She'd grown so used to hoping, to imagining things as she desperately wanted them to be that she could no longer distinguish true sincerity when she heard it. She wanted to look Clark in the eye, but she did not dare.

"I'm...I'm fine." It wasn't a lie, she told herself. It was an affirmation. She *would* be fine. She clamped her jaw tight. She would be more than fine; she would be strong and sure and in control. She had to be. She gulped down the bitterness burning high in her chest and angled her head up, but not her gaze. "It's just that your...your suggestion took me a little by surprise. I expected something—"

"I know what you expected, Becky, and if it were within my ability to offer it to you, I would." The quiet power that rose from his words, from his very being, made her look up. "Believe me, I would."

She wanted to believe him, but how could that be? This man could have or do absolutely anything he wanted—if he wanted it badly enough. That realization cut through her like a knife. Perhaps Clark did want her, care for her even, but only this much and not one compromise more.

There was her reality for her. Slowly, she moved her gaze upward over his grim expression. The smooth planes of his cheeks grew taut and his mouth set in a mask of calm tinged with apprehension. His brow furrowed. In his lap, his tanned, seemingly relaxed fingers gripped the white-knuckled fist of his other hand.

She lifted her gaze to his and her breath caught in the back of her throat.

His eyes shone with a tenderness she did not think she had ever seen in a man before. Tenderness, and something more...loneliness? Longing?

She could not say for sure, but it showed a vulnerability she had never seen in Clark before. She could not have dreamed that up, or wished it there, no matter how hard her overly active imagination had worked. Becky pressed her damp palm to the roughened paint of the swing's arm, but that didn't help to steady her erratic thoughts. She simply could not reconcile the look in those eyes with the cold, businesslike deal this man had just laid out before her.

"I'm not sure you do know what I expected you to say to me today, Clark. I honestly didn't know myself. But I do know it wasn't this...this...mutually messy, not married, not-quite-living-together situation."

"Methodical monogamy."

"What?"

"I like to think of it as methodical monogamy."

"Oh." Becky sat back. Now that her initial shock and upset had begun to subside, she no longer felt like screaming, crying and/or slapping Clark in the face for implying she be a kept woman. She wanted to try to understand this. Once she had a complete grasp of what it was he had in mind, she should deal with it like an adult—*then* she could scream, cry and/or slap Clark in the face if she still felt justified in doing any of those. "Methodical monogamy." She tapped her tennis shoe against the wooden floor. The swing jounced. "But it's not living together and it's definitely not marriage."

"Definitely not marriage. No." He frowned. His eyes looked off into the distance, but Becky had the distinct impression it was the distant past he was searching and not the horizon. He sighed and straightened his expansive shoulders. "If it helps matters any, this is the closest I have ever come, or suppose I ever will come, to proposing marriage, Becky."

How was that supposed to help? she wanted to cry out. It was like being runner-up to nobody. Her cheeks flushed. For one second, she thought of bolting but made herself stay put. She had gotten herself into this with her frivolous fantasies. The only way to combat that was by standing firm and hearing this thing out.

"Let me go over your idea again." She drew a shaky breath, pushed aside the jumble of thoughts and feelings clashing within her and began ticking off on her fingers what she understood so far. "I'd work at your company with an ironclad contract that protected me in case things went awry with our relationship. I earn my own way, realize my full potential and therefore do not feel dependent on you. Furthermore, we live apart, no rings, no vows, no plans for a future. *That* is the closest thing to marriage you can come up with?"

"Yes, that pretty much sums it up."

"I see." Anger stirred within her now and she welcomed it. Anger she could channel into action, use it as a catalyst to make a decision—or to persuade Clark to look at things in another way. Still, she wanted to rein it in, not let anything blunt her renewed grasp on the reality of the situation.

She sighed and cocked her head. Wanting to touch him but afraid that would only muddle her thinking, she folded her hands in her lap, then raised her chin. "Clark, according to the definition you just gave me, you are as close as you'll ever be to getting married with everyone who ever signed an employment agreement with your company!"

"Not quite." He chuckled that low, sophisticated, deep-in-his-chest chuckle that sent a quiver down Becky's spine. "No one who ever signed an employment agreement with my company ever got the kind of guaranteed benefits I'm offering you."

She arched an eyebrow trying to appear far more detached and cool than she felt. "Guaranteed?"

"Guaranteed," he whispered.

She swallowed. Her lips parted, but she could not speak.

Clark edged closer, his already predatory gaze penetrating her facade.

His movement set the swing swaying, sending a ripple of movement through her hips and thighs. His body blocked the gentle breeze, creating a shade that radiated with his body's heat, a shade that gave off no cooling relief. Relief from this kind of thing, even Becky realized, came from more heat, more movement, more than she had ever experienced before in her life.

What had started as hurt and confusion, then worked into anger, now melted into a pool of unnamed emotions. Her skin tingled. A dull ache that she could only describe as intimate hunger, pulsed through her. She wanted to touch this man, to kiss him, to—

"What do you say, Becky? Will you consider my offer?" Clark stroked her cheek with one knuckle.

"I...I'll..." Don't answer, her brain screamed.

Funny, she thought, how her brain sounded like a chorus of Dani, Matt and Mrs. Mendlebaum joining in a firm, moral warning. The jolt of it pulled Becky back from the brink of temptation. She could not trust her heart and body to make this important decision. She had to think about this, weigh the consequences, use her head. That is what would keep her from becoming a perpetual dead-end dreamer like her father. A steady, thoughtful approach to managing her life— even her love life—was her best defense.

"Clark, I don't see how I can make such a momentous decision without all the facts." She sank back into the swing, away from his mesmerizing touch. The chains supporting the swing clattered at her jerking retreat.

He sat forward, his feet anchored wide, stabilizing their seat with a minimum of motion. "I thought I'd spelled out the arrangement very clearly. What *facts* are you missing?"

"You say it like you're taking a business meeting." She laughed.

He didn't.

She pressed her lips shut, fighting the urge to tell herself this was strictly business with him, that it wasn't about feelings and wanting to make an emotional connection. There had to be more. She'd seen it in his eyes, felt it in his kiss. Or had she dreamed that up to? She shook her head. "There's been enough miscommunication between us already, Clark. I need to have this straight in my mind before I can give you any kind of an answer."

"That's wise. Of course." He nodded, then took up her hand. "What more do you need to know?"

Her stunned mind could not form any one specific question, so she asked the simplest, broadest one she could think of. "I guess I need to start with 'Why?'"

Chapter Eight

He would not get emotional. Clark tucked his hands in his pants pockets and adjusted his neck, then his shoulders in a quick jerking motion. His shoes crunched over the gravel of the parking lot as Becky led the way to a walking path. He didn't mind going over his reasons for not believing in marriage, but he refused to delve into his hurtful childhood in the openness of Rosemont House's front porch swing. He wouldn't expose his past like that—and he wouldn't get emotional about it, either.

"The sign says it's only a quarter of a mile to the scenic lookout." Becky glanced back at him. The sunlight gave her hair a hazy, halo effect. "Are you up for it?"

"First bowling, now hiking?" He laughed, not because he found himself amusing but because it had an equalizing effect on the tumult building inside him.

"You're determined to make a sportsman out of me yet, aren't you?"

"Well, it's a heck of a lot nicer thing than what you're trying to make out of *me,* isn't it?" She pursed her lips as if ready to stand her ground if he challenged her assessment, but the twinkle in her eye suggested she would allow this to slide by as a jest if he played along.

"At least I'm trusting enough to assume that what you're doing, you're doing in my best interest." He touched his finger to her chin and grinned. Two could play at double-edged words and mixed messages, he thought. "Lead on to the scenic lookout."

She hesitated, then gave a brisk nod and turned to start down the narrow path.

His gaze lingered over her body, her tanned, muscular legs, her round, firm little behind in fitted denim shorts, her small waist and straight back. "Though what on earth could provide better scenery than what I'm already admiring, I cannot possibly imagine."

"Well, since we are going there to talk and not look—"

"I thought the phrase where you're concerned was look but don't touch," he teased.

"Don't know why you'd think that," she murmured, her face in profile as she picked her way ahead of him on the lush, quiet trail. "I never told you not to touch me."

"And you have no idea how encouraging that simple fact is, sweetheart." As long as she didn't say no, he reasoned, he still had a chance of his position winning out. As long as the romance—the affair—the relationship, he finally settled on in his mind—as long as she did not reject it outright, he still held hope.

He reached out to place his hand on her back. She rewarded him with a smile that would have made him whoop in a show of small victory if not for this stabbing pain still nagging him in his chest.

"Do we have to wait until we reach the lookout or can we start this discussion now?" A twig snapped under Becky's tennis shoe.

"We can start now." He preferred they start now while he had the luxury of telling her his story without having to meet the look of pity and strained sympathy in those beautiful eyes of hers. "Shall I just dive in or is there something more specific you wanted to ask me now that you've had a few minutes to think it over?"

"Well, you're the one accusing me of turning you into a jock—so I say *dive*."

He chuckled, but in the pit of his stomach he could empathize with someone perched on the highest of diving boards about to hurl himself downward into uncertain depths. He couldn't help but wonder how she would react to his painful and pivotal—though not exactly tragic—tale. Would she dismiss his experiences as something he should "get over" or empathize with them and understand how deeply they'd changed his outlook? Would telling her this thing he had never told in total to any other person help her see his vantage point? Would it win her over to his plan for their future?

He had no idea how she would respond. He had no control over it, either, and it scared him a little to know he was taking such an uncalculated risk. The one thing he did know, the thing he could control, was his own emotions and he *would* control them, just as he always did.

"I don't believe in marriage." There. That was a sound, sensible, direct beginning.

"What do you mean you don't believe in it?" Humor and disbelief met in Becky's voice. "It's not like the tooth fairy or something that you can just say 'I don't believe in it.' Marriage is a tangible, significant, even sacred reality for many, many people. You can't simply *not* believe in it—it exists."

"Not for me it doesn't." He clenched his jaw. "The whole concept of finding one person who will meet your needs and desires for an entire lifetime, who will actually give themselves freely to you without a bunch of strings attached and then accept what you give back to them, frailties and all? That happily-ever-after route? It's every bit as much a myth to me as the tooth fairy or any other fairy-tale fantasy."

She tensed noticeably at his last words, or was that the reaction to the culmination of his sentiments?

"But why...?" She didn't look at him, but her hand trembled as she reached for a skinny tree trunk to brace herself as she trudged over a mossy stone. "That is, where did you get such harsh ideas about marriage?"

"Where do any of us get our ideas about things like that?" He easily stepped across the damp gray slab of rock she had just scrambled over. "From observation. From experience. My lessons began as a very young child, watching my parents—or more accurately, *listening* to them."

"Oh." She drew the single syllable out.

Clark wanted to ask, "Is that an 'Oh, I see where you're coming from now and it changes everything' or an 'Oh, you're one of those who blames his every self-indulgence and immaturity on his thwarted childhood?'" Instead, he forced down his apprehension and curiosity and went on.

"I can't remember a time when my parents didn't quarrel." He ducked to avoid an overhanging vine, letting the slick leaves whistle through his fingertips as he swept it aside. He tried to make himself aware of the nuances of the trail, the sounds of birds, the smells of things growing thick in the wooded area—anything to keep himself from thinking too much about what he was saying. "I've been told they were madly in love at some point, and they acted like it. That was before I could remember, though. All I recall are the fights and the tears, the hateful words followed by stony silences."

"Clark, I—"

He cut her off by placing his hand to her back to urge her to keep moving forward. Now that he'd begun his story, stopping was not an option. Neither was looking into Becky's eyes and taking the chance that he'd loosen the choke hold he kept all these years on his very private but personally unproductive emotions.

"To look at my folks, you'd think they had everything. They were attractive, wealthy, educated, had a great house, a thriving business—and me."

She laughed, just like he'd hoped she would.

This wasn't so bad, he thought. He'd get through it just fine.

"You're saying looks can be deceiving?"

"Are you talking about me or my folks?"

She shot him a warning glance.

"Okay, yes, in the case of what my parents' marriage seemed like to the average observer, looks could be deceiving." For a fleeting moment he felt eight years old again, pushing a pillow against his ears to try to blot out his parents' harsh words. He grimaced, then dragged his thoughts back to the present, trying to sound suave and untouched by it all as he joked, "My own looks, by the way, are honest, virtuous, moral and true."

"Not the looks I've caught you giving me!" She grinned at him, then started on her way again.

He sneaked another lust-filled look at her backside as she walked away, then gave a husky laugh in agreement.

"So you're saying your folks presented one image to the world and another at home?"

"I don't think they presented it as much as it just seemed like it ought to all be working out far better than it was. It's not like they had to struggle over life-and-death matters after all, or worry about keeping food on the table or a roof over our heads." He had long since forgiven his parents for their shortcomings, or so he had thought until he realized how hot and angry his tone had become. Still, he could not seem to rein it in as he continued. "And the things they'd fight about—they were just so stupid. Pointless, really. Mom complaining to her friends about Dad's bad habits or Dad not calling if he was going to work late. It was all just a bunch of—"

"Respect." Becky stole a look at him over her shoulder but kept walking.

"What?"

"Those kinds of fights are never about the petty things they seem to be about, Clark. They're about respect."

"Are they?" He paused to ponder the question.

"Well, think about it." She came to a halt under an arch of delicate, pale green leaves and put her hands on her hips. "What if I blabbed to everyone about your bad habits? How would you feel about that?"

"Like you didn't respect me," he grudgingly agreed.

Why hadn't he made this connection before? he wondered. His stomach knotted. Not that this new revelation changed his view of marriage one bit. If anything, it strengthened his position because now he saw another facet to relationships capable of going wrong and ruining everything. He drew his hands into determined fists at his sides.

"That's precisely why I've made it a point all these years…" Just then, he looked up and into Becky's eyes. His intention to dismiss marriage and its ill effects faded on his lips and he smiled, just a little. "That's why I've made it a point all these years not to form any bad habits."

"Oh, no. Nope. You're not kidding me off the track, not this time." She shook her head and her braid flicked over one strong, slender shoulder. "Love is important in a marriage, Clark, but without respect for each other's feelings and what's important to the other partner, well, love wears pretty thin after a while. How'd you ever get to be so old and not figure that one out?"

"Well, I...hey, I'm not *so* old." He closed in the few feet of rocky path between them, then placed his hand on her upper arm. "How'd *you* figure it out, being the sweet young thing you are and all? There's the question."

"Well, unlike your parents, mine seemed to have nothing at all—except a lot of kids, bills, love and respect for each other. That love and respect carried us through when nothing else could. But like your parents, outsiders looking at just the statistics on my mom and dad would've assumed they had every reason not to respect each other."

"How so?"

She bit her lip for a moment and he doubted that she would tell him more, then she sighed and tipped her head down. "Dad was a dreamer. Spent what little money he earned on get-rich-quick schemes and easy-money scams. He was always one sweet deal away from a rocket to the top. That's how he used to put it."

"You've got a little of that in you, don't you? I saw it in you that very first day we met."

She winced as if he'd touched a sore spot.

Clark stroked her arm with the side of his thumb. "I liked that about you. Liked it a lot. You have a way of making things I'd never dreamed possible seem almost..."

She raised her chin. Hope shone in the depths of her eyes.

He dropped his hand and stepped back. Just as swiftly, he changed the subject. "Anyway, I'm sorry about your childhood."

"Oh, it wasn't that bad, really. It was hardest on

Matt, his being the oldest and all. It really embarrassed him, you know, what with Woodbridge being a small town and everybody knowing *everything* about each other.'' She wrapped her arms around herself. ''Absolutely everyone knew we were always broke and that my dad was a financial flake. But you know what else everyone knew about my dad?''

''What?''

She cocked her head, her eyes glistening with unshed tears, and the proudest little smile crept across her full, sweet lips. ''Everybody in Woodbridge also knew that Daddy was my mom's knight in shining armor. She never let anybody doubt that for one minute. And they all knew she was his fair princess, as well. He never let anyone, most of all Mom, forget it.''

''Lucky,'' Clark muttered as he fought back a hollow, enveloping sadness. How he wished his parents had known that kind of respect and admiration for one another. Who was he kidding? His parents had gone on to have pretty happy and successful lives after their divorce. If he felt any regret or longing, it was all his own—for all the things that he had never known, might never know if he didn't convince Becky to at least try things his way before they even considered…their alternatives.

Alternatives? What alternatives? Marriage or never seeing each other again? Those were their only real alternatives to his solution and to him they were merely different paths to the same dead end. Weren't they?

He just wasn't sure any longer. The pangs in his stomach—or was it his chest?—intensified. He

thought about asking Becky if she had any more antacid, but remembering how strangely she'd acted
about it before, and the fact that it had done nothing
to ease his discomfort, made him reconsider. Instead,
he took a deep breath. He could see where the wind-
ing trail emptied out into a grassy clearing up ahead
and he fixed his gaze on that.

"Clark?"

"Hmmm?" He couldn't look at her, not yet. In a
minute, his confusion and pain would subside and
he'd be back in control.

"If things were so bad around your house, why did
your mom and dad stay together?"

The question took his already wobbly hold on his
feelings and rattled it just enough to make his eyes
burn. He shut them—hard. He kept his head turned
away from her. He fought to suppress the memories,
the anguish he had borne for so long. It was such a
small thing, really, so long ago. That was one reason
this was all so hard for him. It was the wound of a
child, and it embarrassed the man he had become.

Bigger men than him had overcome far greater
grief in their personal lives and they never let the
battle scars show—ever. He had lived his whole life
on this premise. He had formed his personal philosophy around it—including his ideas about marriage.
It fueled his determination never to let a woman get
close enough to see that part of him, never to let anyone know his secret unfinished business.

He would not let his guard down now. Pulling his
shoulders erect, he cleared his throat to chase away
any traces of raw emotion that might linger there.
"Both Mom and Dad used to tell me that they only

stayed married because of me. I think they thought that was reassuring in some way to tell me that, but…'' He gritted his teeth.

"Oh, Clark,'' she whispered, stopping on the path to turn and lay her fingers on his arm. "You must have been so scared, so lonely.''

He froze. No one had ever said that about him, ever. He'd worked so hard to prevent anyone from knowing. But Becky had seen it, had known it on some basic level without his telling or showing her. She knew and yet looked at him with the same sweet kindness he always found in her searching eyes.

"So you understand now?'' he asked.

"Yes, I think I do.''

"So, you see why we can't get married?''

"Well, no, I…'' She frowned, bewilderment in her eyes. "Just because things didn't work out well for your parents doesn't mean things can't work out for…other people. It can. It does.''

"Becky, don't you get it?'' He took her by the shoulders and gave them an almost imperceptible shake. His heart ached and his pulse thudded in his temples. All his resolve to keep his emotions in check had failed him. He bent to put his face close to hers, and in what little rasp of a voice he could muster, he drove home the pain of a lifetime of guilt and fear. "Becky, it's my fault. Waiting around for me to grow up kept them perpetually unhappy. I am the reason, the cause, the loose end that prolonged my parents' miserable marriage. I think doing that once in a life-time to someone you love is more than enough.''

He released her and pushed on ahead to the clear-ing, aware of her footsteps close behind him.

"No, Clark. Your parents made some bad decisions, but that was *not* your fault." She swept past him, then turned the toes of her simple tennis shoes just inches from his Italian loafers. "You were a little boy, for heaven's sake, a little boy, not a…what did you call yourself?"

He squinted at the hill Mr. Rose had named a scenic outlook. His outlook did not change. He folded his arms and tensed his jaw. "A loose end. I was the loose end that kept my parents—"

"A dangling thread."

"That's another way of putting it."

"No, that's what you think of me. You said you came back to my apartment because you couldn't stand a dangling thread." She put her hand to her chest. Her eyes darted back and forth; her lips parted then closed as though she were mentally interlocking one piece of the puzzle with another. Then all at once it must have snapped into place because she looked up. "That's it, isn't it? That's what this contractual, almost-as-close-as-marriage nonsense is about after all, isn't it?"

"Yes! Exactly!" She did understand. Now, at last, he felt he had a chance of persuading her, of winning her over to his way to thinking. To having her in his life and in his bed for as long as—

"Why you rotten, selfish, poor-pitiful-me… wienie!" Her cheeks flushed an angry pink. Her mouth opened, shut again, and she made a low, guttural groan, her eyes rolling.

Clark blinked, trying to make sense out of her reaction. "Poor, pitiful…what?"

"Oh, don't get me wrong, Clark. I feel badly about

your childhood. I hurt for you, for the little boy who was made to feel responsible for his parents' mistakes. How awful it must have been for you, thinking that about yourself all this time. I, of all people, appreciate what it's like to carry your family baggage forward into your adult life, believe me.''

"I do. I believe you.'' He did. How could he not? She spoke with such conviction and power. It added a new dimension to his regard for the woman, that she could be so passionate as to move him like this without his knowing why. "I do believe you. I just have no idea what you're getting at.''

"This...this thing you have...this saying you have to have every loose end tied up in your life and yet wanting to stay away from marriage.'' She held her hands out from her sides, then let them fall as if she had just explained it in the simplest detail to him. "Don't you see what that is?''

"It's not wanting to re-create the mess I grew up with,'' he said with quiet conviction.

She shook her head and soft golden curls shimmied around her temples and cheekbones. "Wrong. So wrong.''

For some reason, he believed her. Maybe it was because he'd grown to respect her opinion or maybe because no one had ever had the nerve to stand up to Clark Winstead and tell him he was wrong before. He met her gaze and his heart leaped. Or maybe it was something more.

Whatever the cause, he found himself spreading his hands in a gesture of openness and asking, "Suppose you tell me what it is, then.''

"Oh, I'll tell you.'' Her head bobbed up and down.

She crossed her arms and angled out one hip. "I will tell you. But there is one thing I want to make perfectly clear first."

"What's that?"

"You are no Chester Mendlebaum, my friend."

He scrunched down his brow. "On second thought, maybe you're not the kind of person I need to trust for a personal analysis of my—"

"You are never going to resolve your past fears by avoiding them, Clark."

"I'm listening."

"You want to tie up the loose ends of your heartbreaking childhood, then you'd do better to try to find out how to make a marriage work, not run away from the very thought of it." She lifted her chin and then aimed her piercing glare at him. "When you can look at your feelings as you did this afternoon and then say that you'll take the risk. When you know in your heart that you can do better than your parents did, that your history is not going to deprive you of happiness now—then you will have come full circle, Clark. Until then, if you think anything less will bring you fulfillment, you're just dreaming."

Chapter Nine

"Why marriage?"

Becky, who had let her sudden surge of passion propel her to the overlook and to a large flat rock where she could sit and fume, scowled at Clark as he approached. "What?"

"You got to ask me why," he said, his hands in his pockets, his posture deceptively relaxed despite the almost palpable tension radiating from his body. "Now it's my turn. Why does it have to be marriage with you? Why can't we come to some other compromise? Why am I the only one who must make the concession?"

"I never said it had to be marriage or nothing at all," she said, softly narrowing her eyes against the glare of sunlight on his pristine white shirt. "Frankly, I thought it might be too soon to make that kind of leap and I was certainly willing to consider other...possibilities."

"Don't kid me, Becky. You clearly expected a marriage proposal today." He hit the words hard but didn't seem angry. "Serious" better described it. Serious, reserved, in control.

She tried to respond in kind. "Well, what would you think if a man you had gone away with for the weekend said he had a surprise for you and you saw it was in an elegant little jewelry box?"

"A…" He chuckled. "Well, if I were a girl who had a charm bracelet with an ornament to mark every special occasion in my life, I'd think—"

"A charm." She winced. Of course it was a charm. That made perfect sense, much more sense, if she thought about it, than an engagement ring. Darn that side of her that stirred things up into impossible fantasies. "Oh, Clark, you must think I'm such a ninny to have come up with that idea out of thin air and Mrs. Mendlebaum's advice on matters of marriage. You? Like Chester? Not in a million years."

"My mind tells me that's a compliment, but I hear something disparaging in your tone. Can't I be just a little bit like Chester, whatever that means?" He grinned.

"Well…"

Suddenly, his grin faded. "Why would your neighbor give you advice on marriage? You said you didn't expect a proposal until you saw the jewelry box."

"You caught me." She rolled her eyes. "So, I'm a daydreamer, the kind of girl who throws a penny in every wishing well she comes across, hoping for a little magic in her dreary life." She hung her head and pinched the soft fabric of her crew sock between her thumb and forefinger. "And if that magic doesn't oblige, I sometimes concoct it out of—hey, wait just one goldurn minute!''

"A goldurn minute? Is that Indiana time? I know they don't keep daylight saving time in that part of the state but—"

"I didn't make that up about coming here to consider marriage, Clark. When you invited me to go away with you, you said—"

"Whoa! I never said anything about marriage, Becky. I may not know what to think about this theory you've just thrown at me, about the respect issue and my needing to accept commitment as a means of personal healing, but I do know I never mentioned marriage."

Becky jerked her head up. Her pulse skipped and she studied Clark with tempered optimism. If he didn't know what to think about her conclusions regarding his past, that meant he had not dismissed them outright. If he had not dismissed them outright, that meant he might still be open to the ideas that respect and moving past his parents' mistakes could bring him both closure and happiness.

That one thought spoke so much hope to Becky's weary heart that she practically began to babble out a response. "You never said it. Not exactly, no. But you did say, back at my apartment that you wanted to tie the knot."

"I did?" He stroked his chin.

The fact that he didn't deny it or try to explain it away only fired her enthusiasm. She leaped down from the rock and hurried to him, the quickening sound of her feet—*swish-swish, swish-swish*—in the tall grass underscoring her building excitement. "You mentioned going away together to see if we knew each other well enough to…I can't quote you exactly, but I distinctly recall hearing a term like 'tie the knot.' For some girls I know back in Woodbridge, that would be considered one morally binding and not-too-shabby marriage proposal. It's better than anything Frankie McWurter would've come up with, I assure you."

"Who or what is a Frankie McWurter? And how is it you know how he'd propose marriage?"

"Frankie McWurter is…" Was that her overactive imagination kicking in again or did she detect a hint of jealousy in Clark's demeanor? Jealous? Clark? Over Frankie?

It made her want to laugh. Not only was there no comparison in looks, intelligence or style, but her feelings for the two men were at opposite ends of the spectrum. Just thinking of Frankie gave her the creeps, while thinking of Clark made her feel…

She looked at the man standing before her with concern etched on his gorgeous features. She didn't want to label her feelings for Clark, not yet, not knowing where all this might lead. But she would allow that she cared for Clark. She cared for him deeply, and judging from his behavior right now, and that mysterious pain in his chest that her neighbor had predicted as a precursor to love, Becky suspected he cared for her, too.

"Becky?"

"Hmm?"

His expression became bland, but his eyes searched hers with undisguised curiosity. "You were just about to tell me how well you know this McWurter fellow?''

"I was?" If Mrs. Mendlebaum were here, Becky realized, the older woman would advise her not to give away too much information.

Clark did not have to know, for instance, that romantically, Frankie ranked somewhere between a blind date arranged by your protective older brother and an evening scouring shower grout. Let him wonder a little, Mrs. Mendlebaum would surely say. Give the sensation that could prove to be either heartburn or true love another chance to work its way on the man.

"Frankie is..." Becky smiled and tossed her head in a way she hoped looked vivacious and confident. "Well, let's just say you have your past and I have my—''

"Frankie McWurter?"

She didn't say a word, just let him draw his own conclusions.

Color spotted the hollows of Clark's cheeks. "So, are you saying this guy is the equivalent of the women I've had in my..."

Bed. He didn't say it. A man like Clark would never say a thing like that; he had too much class and discretion. Still, even as he pressed his lips together to finish his question, *that's* the word that rang in Becky's consciousness. What Clark really wanted to know was if she had slept with Frankie.

Becky tipped her head and waited, feeling the tiniest bit wicked by not telling Clark the truth, but since that was one of the few things in her life she had to feel wicked about, she decided to savor it a bit. She angled her chin up and narrowed one eye, daring him to come out and say what they both knew he wanted to say.

"Past," he concluded.

"I don't know any of the women you've had in your past, Clark," she murmured in pouty innocence. "So how could I say?"

She reached for him, her fingertips spreading over the sun-warmed material of his shirt. She supposed she should feel ashamed of herself, playing him along like that, but if it helped him discover the real depths of his feelings for her, was it so very wrong? She wasn't actually lying, just omitting a few details, or simply not saying anything at all.

"You know what I'm asking, Becky. You don't have to know any women from my past to understand what I'm getting at." He shifted his feet, more tentative than impatient.

She had to handle this right if she ever hoped to marry this man. And the part of her carefully practiced in always clinging to reality had to admit she did still hope to marry him—eventually. She tilted her head just so to put her face inches below his. She wet her lips in the best seductive ploy she could manage without breaking into embarrassed laughter and gave an exaggerated shrug. "You know how it is between a man and a woman...."

"Yes, *I* do." He tipped his head in perfect kissing position and laced his arms around her, then with a sudden thrilling movement tugged her body against his. "The question is, do you?"

"Don't tell me that in this day and age you're the

kind of man who expects a girl to remain a virgin until she gets—''

"Don't go there," he warned with an air she could only think of as demanding yet sympathetic. "And to answer your question, no. I don't think a girl should remain a virgin unless that's what she really, really wants for herself. But I think you knew that already."

"I, um, guessed as much." She shut her eyes and for a moment everything became a purely sensual experience. From her wobbling knees to her full, tender breasts she could feel every inch of Clark's body, even through their thin summer clothes. *Every* inch.

She felt her cheeks warm, but she kept her hips pressed to the evidence of his arousal. How easy it would be to let this man make love to her, she thought, how wonderful and amazing. She thought of his words. *I don't think a girl should remain a virgin unless that's what she really, really wants for herself.*

Right now, with Clark holding her like this, the last thing she really, really wanted was to deny herself the pleasure of knowing him fully, frantically, forever.

Forever? In that single word, the dreamer in her met the realist. He had not offered her forever and she had no way of knowing right now if he ever would. She inhaled, taking in the smells of the outdoors and of Clark's skin. The breeze tripped over her burning skin. She sighed and looked at Clark again.

He stroked back her hair and touched the braid on her shoulder. "A woman has just as much right as a man to learn about sexual pleasure and satisfaction, be she virginal or...well schooled in the, um, intimate arts."

"And let me guess—you're in the business of teaching willing participants?" She said it more for herself than for him, to remind herself that for all his plans and proclamations, she really wasn't unique or special in this regard to this man who had probably known many, many women.

"It's more of a hobby, really," he said.

A more sophisticated woman would have laughed. She couldn't. She smiled weakly and started to step back.

Clark caught up her chin to keep her gaze raised to his. He looked deeply into her eyes. "Or, at least, it has been up until now."

Hope stirred inside her. "And what about now?"

"Now I'm thinking of taking up another hobby. Specializing, as it were."

"In?"

His kiss became his answer. A hard kiss, but not brutal, ripe with a longing that went beyond mere physical desire. He wrapped his arms around her and pressed her to him as if he had no intention of ever letting her go.

Becky rose up on tiptoe, unaware until she did of the sheer delight the delicate friction of their clothes and bodies rubbing together would bring.

He cupped one hand behind her head and deepened the kiss. She did not resist. How could she? She wanted that and even more. Her body ached for him as it never had, never could have, for any other man.

He slid his tongue across her lips and she readily opened them to him. His fingers worked their way beneath the hem of her shirt and then her bra, caressing her naked breast with a tenderness that seemed to border on reverence. She leaned into his touch, welcoming that, too.

He groaned aloud, breaking off contact for only a second before smothering her mouth again in smaller, even more urgent kisses. "I want you, Becky."

"I want you, too."

"Why can't that be enough?" he pleaded.

"Why can't there be more?" she whispered.

He tensed. His mouth remained poised over hers for the length of time it took him to search her eyes and realize they had reached the point of compromise.

"What if I said that there could be?"

Joy exploded in her heart.

"Someday," he added, his brows angled down and his expression dark as if he were wading against a tide of emotional confusion.

Her joy dimmed.

"Maybe." Hoarseness edged his tone.

He'd gone as far as he could; she saw that in his eyes, his posture, even in the way he loosened his hands on her waist.

For a moment, she saw in him that little brokenhearted boy who could not trust himself to commit to love again. But even her empathy for that boy could not overcome the fears of the little girl in her, the one who continued to dream of Cinderella and happily-ever-afters. She bit her lower lip and found it still tender from his thorough kissing.

"Becky? Say something." It was not a plea but a quiet, powerful bidding for her to give him an answer.

"I...I don't know what to say, Clark. I wish...I wish... No wait." She forced herself to meet his gaze and say what was in her heart before she lost her nerve. "That's not true, Clark. I do know what to say. I only hesitated because I wish there was another way and that very thing—that wishing that somehow the reality of this situation could change—"

"I just told you they might. That's as much as I can give right now, Becky."

He reached for her.

She took a step backward, her head shaking. "Yes, and by doing that, Clark, you've asked me to live my life in a state of perpetual dreaming—always hoping for the day when my real desires would come true. Yearning for the day when I could become your wife and maybe have some children."

"I want children, too," he said softly.

"You do?" Her breath caught high in her chest. She blinked, wondering if every conversation with Clark about their relationship would always feel like such a wild roller-coaster ride. "Well, if you want kids, then you must think that someday you'd have to get—"

He put his hand on her arm to stop her before she could even say the word. "That's the beauty of my plan. I've made a provision for children, all the legal necessities to grant them the rights of legitimate heirs without…to accomplish that under these special circumstances. Your brother's a lawyer. He can look over the details and assure you everything is in proper order."

Becky blurted out a soft laugh. "The only 'proper order' my brother would support for our having children is 'first comes love, then comes marriage, *then* comes Becky with a baby carriage.'"

"It's your life you have to think about, not his," he said softly.

"Not in this case. In this case, it's our children's lives I have to think about first and foremost."

"I knew that about you," he murmured almost as if to himself. His eyes glittered with pride and enthusiasm. "You're going to be an excellent mother."

The compliment tore at her already raw emotions. She stepped back again, as if physical distance from him could keep the crush of her own feelings at bay. "Yes, I believe I am going to be a good mother, but not under those circumstances. I won't have children without putting their needs first. And they need both parents if at all possible."

"Don't you see that's what I'd be trying to insure them? Two parents who will always be available for them, who will not be caught up in petty bickering and self-involvement. Two separate, strong individuals, who are their parents by design not duty." His jaw clenched tight as he spoke and his breathing grew hard and measured. "Parents who can never divorce because they never made the mistake of marrying in the first place."

"Parents who by their own selfish actions have chosen to perpetuate the pain of both their own childhoods," she added with trembling dignity. "No, Clark, I won't do that. I can't. You've offered me a lot—Cinderella gets to go to the ball and have everything she ever dreamed of except the one thing she really wants with all her heart. I guess if we were just talking glass slippers, I'd say it was a pretty good fit. It would at least be worth the try. But when you start talking baby shoes..."

She stepped back again, the sight of Clark's perplexed face blurred by her tears.

"It's not fair," she choked out. She turned on her heel and, sniffling, began to jog toward the path that had led them to the overlook.

"Becky, where are you going? Come back."

She didn't answer. She broke into a run. Midnight, Cinderella, she told herself, and the harshness of the real world had shattered her illusions. But unlike the fairy tale, there would be no magical ending to make her dreams come true. Her dreams were as good as dust as long as Clark felt the way he did.

"Becky? Becky, open up." Clark pounded on the door to her room. He hadn't gone after her when she had run off because they both needed the time to think, to collect themselves, to get their libidos and their feelings back under control.

He'd gone for a walk. He'd taken a shower. He'd dressed for dinner. He'd tried to spend that time thinking about what had gone on between them, to make sense of it all. But the more he thought, the stronger the pain in his stomach had gotten. He couldn't concentrate, couldn't come to any definite, useful answers.

Glass slippers? Baby shoes? He just didn't see the correlation any more than she seemed to see his point of view. He needed to talk to Becky, he decided, to finish this discussion once and for all so that they could both move on in whatever direction it took them, together or apart.

"It's been two hours. That's long enough to sulk," he said, knocking again. "We have to talk."

Silence.

"Oh, c'mon, Becky. Let's be civil about this, or at least practical. You can't spend the rest of the weekend locked in your room. It isn't a hotel. You'll have to come out to eat and when you do it might as well be with me."

Real romantic, Winstead. No wonder she ran off, he chided himself now that he'd cooled off some and could actually listen to the way he presented things to her. Had he sounded so formal and pragmatic when he'd asked her to be the only woman in his heart, his bed and his life for as long as she could stand him?

He hung his head and sighed. He knew he had. What a fool! He'd treated the whole thing like a buyout and not an equitable merger. Then he'd committed a greater mistake, letting his emotions override his finely honed instincts.

He was a far better salesman than that. He knew how to handle the most delicate of negotiations; he could dazzle the most jaded of businessmen. He could charm absolutely anyone if he so desired—then plant his flag on them and claim them in the name of the Winstead Corporation, as his old pal Baxter would say. But not Becky.

He laughed despite the ache in his chest and the fog in his mind. Becky was one of a kind. A gem. A treasure. A charm.

"A charm," he muttered as his hand dipped into his pants pocket to retrieve the small jeweler's box. That might just do the trick. It would not salve all the hurt that his calculated approach had caused her, but it would be a good start to put them back on track. Clark was the kind of man who got what he wanted, and right now he wanted to talk things over with Becky Taylor once and for all.

He knocked on the door again. "Open the door, Becky, please. I never had the chance to give you the charm I bought for your bracelet. I'd really like for you to have it and see if we can't—"

"She ain't there, son," Mr. Rose said, rounding the corner from the stairwell. "Heard you kicking up a fuss at her door and figured I'd best come tell you. She didn't leave no note or message for you specific. She did ask me to tote up the bill for the weekend and send her a copy so she could pay you her fair share, that's all. She's been gone a good twenty minutes."

"Gone?"

"Called that brother of hers—the one who was up here before—and he come and got her." Mr. Rose, a gnarled string bean of a man who looked better suited to tending livestock than live-in guests, shoved his weathered hands into the deep pockets of his bib overalls. "Looked like she'd been crying, too. Not that that's any of my business."

"I...see." Gone? She'd left him? No one had ever left him. No employee, no business associate, no lover. When the split came, it was always his decision or by mutual design.

"Heard her tell that brother she was a-moving home for good, then she garbled out something about baby shoes." The older man squinted hard at Clark, a kind of wordless accusation that he might have gotten Becky pregnant, then planned to abandon her.

Clark had to laugh. The old man could not have been further off the mark. He had never even made love to Becky, much less a baby with her—and if he had done either, he knew in his heart that he could never have walked away from her. Now she'd walked away from him.

The one thing he had hoped to avoid with all his careful machinations had happened—and happened because of his effort to manipulate his own brand of happy ending. While he could appreciate the irony, Clark knew it would be a long time before he could look back and laugh at it. A very long time.

Still, better that it happened now, he told himself, before he really had fallen hopelessly in love with the girl. What he felt for her now was...

The pain in his chest tightened.

What he felt now was that he had probably developed an ulcer over the whole ordeal. Nothing that couldn't be eased by a good doctor and a no-holds-barred, no-commitments-expected...date with an open-minded woman.

He'd wasted enough time and effort over something completely nonproductive. He had work to do and women to woo. This chapter of his life was concluded, the loose thread unraveled to its very last stitch.

"Thank you for telling me, Mr. Rose. I'll be checking out now—paying for both rooms for the entire weekend, of course."

"Gonna go after her, son?"

"On the contrary, Mr. Rose, I'm going to run, not walk, in the opposite direction. As far as I'm concerned, Miss Taylor and I have drawn a line of demarcation between us. She gets Woodbridge, Indiana, a house with a picket fence and all the baby booties she can hang on a bracelet.''

Mr. Rose scratched his head in obvious confusion. "And me?'' He plunked his hand on the innkeeper's bony shoulder, ignoring the man's befuddled look. "I get the rest of the world and the rest of my life to do with as I see fit. I think there are still a few opportunities out there where I haven't already planted my flag.''

Chapter Ten

"I can't believe you did this for me, Mrs. Mendle-baum." Becky had rushed out of her brother's house just in the nick of time to prevent the older woman from hauling a huge cardboard box out of the trunk of the Mendlebaums' land yacht of a car. "Here, let me take that. You've gone to enough trouble already."

"What trouble?" Mrs. Mendlebaum batted her hand in the air, and a cloud of stiflingly floral perfume went wafting in Becky's direction. "When you called to tell me you weren't coming back to your apartment, I was happy to gather up your things. It's not so many things, you know, since you rented furnished."

"Uh-huh." Becky staggered under the weight of the box. "Actually, it feels like quite a lot. Are you sure you only packed my things? It should only be the clothes, the toiletries and a few photograph albums and knickknacks. This..." She paused to get a better grip on the heavy box. Things clinked, clattered and rustled, then something slid to one side with a hard clunk. "This feels like a lot more."

"Oh, that." Mrs. Mendlebaum tipped up her nose, relieving her round face of at least one of her many chins, and sniffed. "Don't you worry about that. Since you said you didn't have a job yet, I made a few things. Some turkey, a few cakes, a pie."

"Oh, my, Mrs. M, you shouldn't have!" Becky meant that with all sincerity—she'd tasted her ex-neighbor's cooking before. "You really shouldn't have cooked for me, especially not after you volunteered to drop these things off on your way to visit your son in Cincinnati."

"Just a smidge out of our way. A trifle. Nothing really." Mrs. Mendlebaum slammed the trunk shut with such force it made the entire car bounce. Her husband, who sat inside the car, didn't even look up from the newspaper held open before his face. "Okay, so it was an hour off the road from our trip. Big deal. I don't mind. Chester doesn't mind."

"At least let me invite you in for some iced tea and a bite to eat or something."

"No, please, we couldn't." Mrs. Mendlebaum fumbled with the sturdy silver man's wristwatch she wore on a gold chain around her neck. Looking as if she smelled something truly awful, she peered at the watch face from a spot just under her nose, then extended her arm back and forth like a trombone player until a smile broke over her features. "We're on a tight schedule. If we get off it by even one half hour, Chester will be impossible to live with."

Becky indulged in a quick smile at that, then raised her knee to try to balance the box, which seemed to be growing heavier the longer they tarried in Matt's driveway. "But I want to do something. This was a huge favor."

"What favor? I *wanted* to do it." She pinched Becky's cheek. "Don't ask me again about repaying or I'll take it as an insult, you understand? You are such a good girl. A good neighbor. If my son in Cincinnati wasn't already married—"

"Still…" Becky leaped in so abruptly that she lurched forward, making the contents of the box shift. She compensated with a stumbling side step. "I'd like to repay you in some way."

"You repay me by inviting me to the wedding, maybe name a daughter after me—wouldn't have to be a first name, mind you, I'm not greedy, but—"

"I can't."

"Can't what, invite me? It's going to be a private ceremony?"

"There isn't going to be any ceremony. In fact, I'm never going to see Clark again. It's over."

"Over? No. No, it's not over. When you talked about this man, I could see in your face how much you loved him."

"Yes. Yes, I did love him. I still do." That was the first time she'd admitted it aloud—not that she thought saying it to Clark would have changed his opinion about marrying her. If anything, it might have sent him scurrying away even faster and farther than he'd already gone. Imagine him trying to cope with the concepts of respect, commitment, emotional maturity and *love* in one demanding, challenging, ridiculously outclassed package—her? She shook her head. "But it wasn't enough. It never could be. He just didn't feel the same way that—"

"Huh!" Mrs. Mendlebaum snorted. "He felt those pains?"

"Well, yes, he did, but—"

"He took the medicines?"

"Yes, at least, I saw him take one, once."

"And the pains? They didn't get better, right?"

"I…I don't know. I didn't ask."

"You didn't ask? I told you this was important. Did I not tell you it was important?" She rapped on the side of the box with each syllable like a teacher drilling an errant student.

Becky clamped her fingers more tightly on the bottom of the box, trying to keep the other woman from jarring the cumbersome thing loose from her hands and doing who-knows-what kind of damage. "Well, yes, you told me it was important, but so much happened—"

"Young people," Mrs. Mendlebaum said, throwing up her hands. "You have no follow-through, no patience to stick with something to the bitter end."

"Oh, it got bitter enough in the end, don't worry about that." Becky's lips twitched into a humorless smile. "But that's all behind me now. Now I have to concentrate on my future and hope I don't make the same mistake with—"

"Hey, Beck! Heads up!" Frankie McWurter brought his father's tow truck to a screeching halt nose-to-nose with the Mendlebaums' car.

Becky flinched, tipping the box to one side, then righting it again.

Mrs. Mendlebaum gasped, then scowled. Then her eyes widened like a jeweler sizing up a diamond in the rough as Frankie leaped from the truck's cab and came striding toward them.

Through it all, from behind the steering wheel, Chester Mendlebaum's newspaper did not even flutter.

Frankie bounded right up to them, his work-blackened nails scratching at the five-o'clock shadow he'd taken five days to produce. "Hey, Beck, saw you as I drove by and—"

"Not now, Frank. If you haven't noticed, I'm a little preoccupied here."

He wiped his hand across his blue-and-white-striped shirt, right over the patch that bore his older brother's name. "Yeah, that's why I came up. I thought you could use some help."

Didn't she feel like a perfect jerk? The first time she'd seen Frankie in the two weeks she'd been back in Woodbridge and she immediately assumed the worst. Ill-fated romance certainly had not improved her people skills, she chided herself.

"Thanks, Frank." She heaved her burden high against her chest, ready to unload it into Frankie's waiting arms. "I really could use a—"

He had vanished.

Becky made a last-minute save, clutching hard to protect her belongings from a sudden drop to the driveway. "Frankie?"

"What?" He literally popped up in front of her.

She gasped, then recovered her senses. "I thought you were going to help me."

"I did. See?" He held up the red oil-soaked cloth

that usually dangled from his pants pocket. "Something from that box was dripping on the driveway. I'm not sure, but it looks like gravy."

"My specialty!" Mrs. Mendlebaum flung her hand to her chest as though the accident had dealt her a deathblow.

"Pure grease," Frankie said, and Becky wondered how he'd known that without having tasted the fatty, lump-filled mixture. "You gotta get a stain like that up right away. Otherwise it sets in the surface and you can't hardly sandblast it out."

That's exactly how she felt about the stuff, Becky thought. She inched over far enough to set the box in the grass where any toxic leakage might actually do some good by killing a few weeds, then straightened. "Well, thanks for everything, Frankie."

"No, thank *you.* I bet you thought I forgot about this." He wriggled his fingers into the back pocket of his skintight pants, then produced a crumpled twenty-dollar bill. "You loaned me this before you went off to Chicago. Don't never let it be said that Franklin W. McWurter doesn't pay his debts. And with interest."

He leaned over and gave Becky a peck on the cheek as he poked the money into her hand.

Mrs. Mendlebaum's eyebrows registered real surprise at that.

"I'd give you more, but the bank-o-Frank's good lovin' is now officially closed to the public." Frankie stepped back with both his hands up. "I'm getting married two weeks from Saturday."

"Frankie! That's so—"

"You come." He pointed directly at Becky as he took one step backward.

"Frankie, I don't know what my—"

"Say yes." He began walking backward, his finger still trained on her. "You gotta say yes because you know the Frankmeister don't take no for an answer. Tell me you'll be there or I may not be able to go through with it. Unless, of course, you want me back on the market so you can have me all to your—"

"Yes! Yes, I'll be there. I promise."

He laughed and waved goodbye. The tow truck groaned into gear and in a moment he was gone.

Becky turned to Mrs. Mendlebaum, jerked her thumb over her shoulder in Frankie's general direction and said, "And to think Clark Winstead was jealous of *him*."

"He was? Mr. Good Sport jealous of...of—"

"Jealous of the idea of him, of that fact that I had dated him. Clark never actually met Frankie. I just told him a tiny bit about the two of us and he drew his own conclusions."

"Enough said."

Becky wondered what caused the peculiar, knowing smile on her ex-neighbor's face. She chose not to pursue it, figuring it could denote anything from a wild notion she'd rather not hear about to a case of trapped gas.

"Frankie's nothing to me. That's why I didn't introduce you. The less people who come into contact with that part of my past, the better, I think."

"Perfectly understandable, my darling."

"And besides, I knew you had to get on your way again—unless you've changed your mind and you and Chester want to come in. I feel so badly that your husband is just sitting in that car. Wouldn't he want to come in just to cool off?''

"Chester? The poor thing! You couldn't drag him out from that car. He says all this fresh air makes him nauseous." She offered a tight smile toward the newspaper, which suddenly rustled briskly in Mr. Mendlebaum's knobby fingers. "But you're right. We do have to get going again. Our schedule, you know."

"I'm so grateful for everything you've done." Becky motioned toward the box on the lawn, saw an oozing brown stain on one corner and remembered the cakes, pie, turkey—and whatever remained of the gravy. "I'll mail back your food containers as soon as we've emptied them."

Into the garbage, a wicked little voice in her wanted to add.

"No need." Her friend waved off the offer. "I sent everything in plastic bags."

"Oh. How convenient," she said through a plastered-on smile. Suddenly, she felt compelled to hurry this goodbye along so she could get inside that box and get her belongings cleaned up before she needed a sandblaster to do so as Frankie had suggested. "Um, well, thank you again so very much for bringing my things."

"You're very much welcome. Is there anything else we can do?"

"Anything else? My, no, you've done so much—"

"We are going back to Chicago, you know. It would be no trouble to take something with us. If there was something you'd want to send back...a message to...oh, a certain good sport, perhaps?"

"No. No, Mrs. Mendlebaum. There's nothing I want to say to him." Her breathing shortened even as the lie left her lips. She wanted to say everything to him, beginning with "I love you" and ending with—no, never ending at all. But this man liked his endings, liked things all neatly tied up and finished off. She'd had her chance with him. She'd made her choice. That part of her life was done and she had to face it. "No, there's nothing I want to send him."

"You are sure?"

Becky clasped her hands together. The supple twenty-dollar bill compressed between her palms. Her promise to pay him back rang in her mind and she jerked her head up. "Wait. There *is* something you could do. I planned to send him this in the mail, and after this first one that's what I'll have to do, but now while everything is still so…fresh for me, I'd rather have a go-between. I wouldn't ask, but his office is so close to our building—to *your* building."

Becky wet her lips. She'd begun babbling. She did that when an idea seized her like this. She'd done a lot of it around Clark, from that very first day when he'd taken her charm and given her his business card.

"Hang on a second. I have his card I can give you." She took two lunging steps to the box, ripped it open and peered inside. Luckily, her jewelry box, the place she kept all her most treasured possessions, was safe and dry on top. In a matter of seconds, she had pulled out the card and turned back to Mrs. Mendlebaum. "You won't have to take it to him personally. Just drop it in an envelope at this address."

Becky held the card close, clasped in both hands for only a moment before handing it over. As the fine paper left her fingers, she said her silent goodbyes to Clark and the dream he had represented then crushed.

"Money? You want I should give *that* man money? Becky, money he's got. What he needs is—"

"He needs an ending. To tie up the loose threads. And I need to show him that I try to live my convictions about respect and maturity and facing one's past in order to move forward."

"You want I should tell him that?" She looked slightly panicked.

"Don't tell him anything, really." Becky laughed, but her aching heart wasn't in it. "He'll know what it's for. He'll know it's my first payment on an unwise investment. He, of all people, will understand that it's important to this Cinderella that she buys her own glass slippers and doesn't wait around for a prince who may never come to do it for her."

"What's that?" Baxter pointed to the limp twenty-dollar bill that feisty old Mrs. Mendlebaum, who had just marched in, plunked on the desk.

"Payback, my friend, in every sense of the word." Clark rubbed the bill between his thumb and forefinger, his thoughts touching only an instant on the fact that Becky had once held this in her hand. The image of the girl with the golden curls and the lopsided glasses as he'd first seen her came to his mind and he smiled. He hadn't smiled in weeks, he realized.

"If you are as smart as you are rich and handsome, you'll know this isn't about money, Mr. Winstead. You'll know what Becky is really saying with this." Mrs. Mendlebaum pursed her lips.

Clark smoothed the pad of his thumb over the soft bill.

"Ah! It's the girl." Baxter's face lit up. His broad smile took on a smug angle. "She didn't just refuse to be claimed by the Winstead charm-and-money expedition. She's throwing you off the whole mountain, isn't she?"

"In installments." Clark laid the money on the desk and leaned back.

Baxter hooted out a laugh.

"I thought you'd enjoy that." Even Clark could appreciate the humor of a man of his wealth and status being rebuffed in small, never-ending increments. Only Becky could do that to him and pull it off as her own personal triumph and not as a means of ridiculing him. At once he felt both proud of her and ashamed of himself for letting her go.

He'd thought a lot about what she had said regarding his parents and the decisions he'd made because of them. Her words made sense. They made him feel that perhaps he could look at things differently, and given enough time, maybe he could see things her way. Maybe.

If she hadn't left him, he might have tried to explore those options further, but now it was too late. That was past tense. Over.

He'd put her completely out of his mind—out of his wakeful mind, he corrected, out of the part of his mind over which he could maintain strictest control. At night, though, his dreams turned to her, igniting anew the burning desire to hold her, to kiss her, to claim her body with his and make her his alone.

Those would pass, he told himself. He'd find a way

to put them aside. Just as he had put aside the thoughts and memories of her that caught him off guard during his workday, his tennis games, even the one miserable excuse for a dinner date he'd attempted this past month.

He had his conscious thoughts entirely within his control—until, of course, today, when this little reminder had blindsided him. He wadded the twenty into his fist and battled back the twinge of pain starting to build in his chest again. With a gargantuan effort, he bent his grimace into a smile for the older woman with towering hair, too much perfume and a man's wristwatch on a chain around her neck, who sat facing him across the expanse of his desk. "Thank you for bringing this to my attention, Mrs. Mendlebaum."

"You're quite welcome, I'm sure." She gave a little bow as though she were addressing royalty, but her expression was that of someone smelling a sewer rat.

He deserved that, he supposed. He'd hurt her friend. He'd hurt the only woman he could ever... Something essential within him baited him to finish the thought, though he didn't want to even think the word. Not now, not after it was too late.

Love. He felt it as much as thought it. He knew it and understood it all in one flashing moment. And in that moment, he knew how much he'd truly lost, the price he had finally paid for not dealing with the pain of his childhood.

"Mrs. Mendlebaum, is it?" Baxter held out his hand to the woman. "Baxter Davis, college friend and trusted adviser to Mr. Winstead."

"A pleasure." She pumped his hand up and down as if she were priming for water.

Clark used the distraction of their introductions to clear away his unproductive thoughts and regain his composure before he spoke. He even managed a wry smile and a bit of a chuckle as he explained, "Mrs. Mendlebaum used to be Becky Taylor's neighbor here in Chicago. She insisted on delivering Becky's payment to me in person because she didn't feel right handing over such a large sum of money to my secretary."

"Miss Harriman?" Baxter blinked as though unable to even comprehend the suggestion. "Why, I'd trust her with my life."

"Not to offend, young man, but my dear little Becky entrusted this money to me along with a very important, highly personal message. I should give those to just any old body sitting behind a fancy-schmancy desk?"

"No, ma'am. I see your point entirely." Baxter patted her back, his tone and attitude that of a kindred spirit in the matter. "You did the right thing, coming directly to Mr. Winstead to give him...a *message* did you say? May I be so bold as to ask what kind of message—asked strictly from the vantage point of Clark's closest friend and adviser, of course."

Mrs. Mendlebaum arched one eyebrow at Clark, no small feat given the already perilous peak to which she'd drawn the thing onto her brow.

He nodded, granting her his silent permission to restate the cryptic message she said she'd gotten from Becky almost two weeks ago.

"She said she had to show some respect and that

she has convictions from moving in the past and that she wanted Mr. Winstead should have this money even though he's not coming around anymore and she probably should have bought shoes with it.''

Baxter opened his mouth, ready to make a joke and/or laugh in the woman's face for her ludicrous mishandling of whatever Becky had said.

Clark cleared his throat and, when he had Baxter's eye, shook his head. He would not stand by and let anyone disparage a person who, despite her confusion, obviously cared so much for Becky.

"Shoes, you say?" Baxter tilted his head to one side as if fascinated. "Why do you suppose she would need to buy shoes?"

"Beats me." The woman vastly overplayed a shrug but didn't hesitate long enough to make her ploy seem realistic when she looked a little too casually out the window and said, "Maybe it's for the wedding."

"Wedding?" Baxter glanced at him.

"What wedding?" Clark scowled. He recognized manipulation when he saw it, but he also understood this woman wanted nothing from him. Her only goal in getting involved, he had quickly surmised, was her concern for Becky. Knowing this not-so-subtle hint she'd just torpedoed into the conversation was her way of showing that concern made him both anxious and suspicious at the same time. "You never mentioned a wedding before."

"Did I say wedding?" Mrs. Mendlebaum covered her mouth with her hand. "Oh, my, I hope I haven't said something I'm not supposed to."

Mrs. Mendlebaum was never going to win any acting awards. Clark's suspicions eased; whatever she was up to, he trusted this woman had Becky's interests at heart. She simply wasn't a slick enough operator to be trying to pull one over on him for any other reason.

"I want you should know about the wedding? That wasn't a part of the message. Becky did not say for me to tell you that or about that fellow I saw her with."

"What fellow?" Clark leaned forward.

"Frank? Frankolyn? Frankmeister?" She tapped her chin with each variation.

"Frankie?" Clark asked.

"Yes, that's it! Frankie MacWurlitzer." She clapped her hands together, then stood. "So much for that. The wedding's next Saturday. Now, I have to be on my way."

Like an uncapped gusher, the wild mix of Clark's emotions shot through him. He bolted up from his chair, his fist slamming down atop the twenty he'd just been given. "Becky is marrying Frankie McWurter?"

"I don't think it's wise for me to be discussing the particulars about this wedding with you, Mr. Winstead." Mrs. Mendlebaum glanced around the room. Then, seemingly satisfied that Becky had no spies lurking about, she leaned over the desk and said in a stage whisper that would rattle the rafters if Clark had had any, "But I was there and I did hear him say he would not take no for an answer."

"So she said yes?" Baxter asked before Clark could say anything more.

"You didn't hear it from me, but..." She put her hand over her heart, looked upward as if gathering strength, committed herself to go on, then announced, "As God is my witness, she told the man yes to the Saturday wedding."

Clark turned to look out the window, the same window he'd spotted Becky from on that first day. He swallowed hard. "Awfully damned fast, isn't it? Just a month ago, she wanted to marry me, and now she's ready to spend her life with someone else, ready to go off with him and…"

The image exploded in his mind—Becky making love with someone else. Someone else's hands on her, someone else losing himself in her, body and soul.

The pain in Clark's chest became a raging fire. He clamped his jaw down tight as he admitted—finally— to himself—that he'd give anything to be that man. *Anything*.

But could he *give up* anything? Because that's what it would take. Could he let go of the past, of his fears and mistrust? He shut his eyes tight.

If he could do that, had it all come just too damn late? If he could make that leap of faith and try to be the man—the husband—Becky needed him to be, would she still marry this McWurter fellow?

"When you say Saturday—" Baxter's voice cut through Clark's internal deliberation and brought him back to the immediate situation "—do you mean Saturday, a week from tomorrow, or Saturday, tomorrow?"

"A week."

Clark blew out a long breath, turned back around and opened his eyes again. At least that gave him time, time to think this through and then take action if he felt it was the absolute right thing to do.

"No, wait."

Clark jerked his head up.

"We were in Cincinnati ten days, so we saw Becky on the…" Mrs. Mendlebaum's head bobbed back and forth and up and down as though she were counting the days on an invisible calendar. Then she went still, looked directly at him and gave a brisk nod. "Tomorrow. The wedding is tomorrow."

"Tomorrow?" He shouted the word like a man on the verge of losing control. Catching himself, he straightened his tie and took a deep breath. If Becky wanted to get married so badly she'd take up with some yahoo of an old boyfriend, who was he to be upset by it? She had that right. And unless he was willing to lay everything he'd ever believed in on the line and offer himself as a marriage partner instead, he had no right to object. Even if he did, why should she want him now? She had moved on with her life and gotten what she wanted most.

Clark cocked his head, his voice low and cultured when he spoke again. "Well, thank you for telling me, Mrs. Mendlebaum, and if you see Becky, please convey to her my wishes for her every happiness with…" The name lodged in his throat and would not come out. "Please convey my wishes for her happiness."

Mrs. Mendlebaum glared at him, shook her head, muttered something about young people, then started for the door. With each step, her grumblings became louder and more pronounced. "Happiness! Ha! What would you two know from happiness? Both of you with your fancy talk about not making the same mistakes your parents did—baloney. If nobody ever made the same mistakes their parents did, we'd none of us be here today.''

Clark smiled to himself at the logic of that.

''And meanwhile, while you two are trying so hard to avoid the misery you went through growing up, you both make your own whole new brand of misery for yourselves.''

That logic wiped the smile off his face. He hung his head, then something occurred to him. ''*Both* of us miserable? Why would Becky be miserable if she's getting married? She's getting what she wants, isn't she?''

''Is she? You tell me.'' The older woman took another step, her skinny high heels wobbling just a bit on the thick carpet. Just before she reached the door, she stopped and looked back, this time dropping all the pretense and bad drama. ''Myself, I have to wonder, why does a girl who is through with a man care so very much about what he thinks of her that she'd take her last few dollars to repay a debt that only she believes she really owes?''

Clark's heart beat faster as he considered that.

''And while you're at it, also tell me why a man who doesn't think marriage is such a big deal gets so upset to learn that the girl he turned down is marrying someone else. By your calculations, Mr. Winstead, Becky will be divorced and back on the market in no time, and probably a little jaded in the process and more accepting of your way of thinking on the subject.''

''No. Not Becky. If Becky marries someone, anyone, she will make it work. She may be a bit of a dreamer, but she's not *just* that. She's someone who goes after her dreams and does all she can to make them come true and…'' The pain in his chest seemed to change into a cold lump that fell to the pit of his stomach. He ground out a curse between his teeth at his own ignorance and arrogance. Why hadn't he seen this before?

He pressed the heel of his hand to his forehead, his head bent, and allowed himself a mirthless chuckle. "Okay. You win, Mrs. Mendlebaum. Baxter, can you help Miss Harriman defer any appointments I have this afternoon?"

"Why? Where are you going to be?"

"I have a few things to take care of first and then I'm on my way to Woodbridge, Indiana."

Chapter Eleven

The thick scatterings of birdseed on the church steps crunched beneath Becky's heels as she stood alone in the aftermath of Frankie McWurter's wedding. She shimmied one hand through her hair trying to dislodge some of the teeny insidious granules Frankie's nephew had "accidentally" pelted her with. A Woodbridge town ordinance prohibited the throwing of rice at weddings for the sake of the birds, but it gave no consideration to the people who had to deal with the stuff.

She decided she'd just worked the seeds down closer to her scalp at this rate, so she pulled her fingers free of the knotty nest she'd created. She sighed and tried to give a quick fix to the neat French twist she'd worked so hard on this morning, only to find she'd worked half of it loose enough to leave a curtain of golden curls straggling along her neck and temple and down her back.

She glanced down at her pink suit, the one she had worn on job interviews in Chicago, the one she had on the day she met Clark, then looked around her. Everything was quiet. The wedding party had gone on to the reception now, as had all the guests and the photographer—everyone but her. She just couldn't face it—a hall full of people she'd known her whole life, all asking her the same thing. "So, Becky, when is it going to be you?"

"When?" she heard herself whisper without intending to ask it aloud. She felt numb to her surroundings and aware only of her sense of loss and longing, both caused by the very same man. She tipped back her head to take in the sight of the simple little white church, the door still draped in wedding tulle and finery. Her throat grew tight, her heart heavy. Tears filled her eyes, but her thoughts filled with the question she asked again. "When?"

Someday. Clark's tentative concession echoed in her mind. *Maybe.*

"And maybe never," she murmured because she needed the staunch reminder. She could never let herself forget that all Clark offered was the fantasy of a relationship, one without substance, without commitment.

If only he'd shown just one little sign, though, the dreamer in her had to assert. One sign that he was open to change, that he was willing to compromise, to work together, to give just a little, and she would have stayed. Stayed? No power on earth could have made her leave.

After all, she wasn't unreasonable or unyielding herself. She raised her chin, shut her eyes and let the late-morning sun warm her damp cheeks. The sounds of cars coming and going on one of the busiest streets in her small town became muted by her own drive to reaffirm her choices concerning Clark.

She had not been too hasty or inflexible, she told herself. She had never had any overwhelming desire to rush into marriage before both of them were ready. She had just wanted to know that their relationship had that potential, that they had a future beyond the bedroom and, in light of Clark's job offer, beyond the boardroom. When she learned that, to Clark, they most likely didn't…

The old pain she thought had begun to heal this past month slashed through her again, full and potent as it had been that first day. She caught her breath and held it, struggling to try to find some kind of comfort in the cold justifications she'd chosen over her own short-term happiness.

Clark was the one who led her to believe that he had a proposal in the works, she told herself. Blame him and his talk of tying knots and promising surprises with a jewelry box in his hand for the way things played out. She hadn't even been in the market for a husband when she'd stumbled across Clark—or more precisely when he'd stumbled across her wayward charm.

She reached down to touch the bracelet circling her wrist, fingering through the miniature mementos by rote until she found the one that now held so much more emotional significance to her than any of the others. All her pride and rationalizations fell away the moment she tugged at that tiny replica of a baby bootie to single it out from the others. She rolled the charm between her thumb and forefinger, replaying in her mind the way it had twice brought her and Clark together.

Third time's a charm. She managed to smirk at the spontaneous reaction to the connection between a charm and a two time loser with that unlikely cliché. For them, there would be no third time. Clark Winstead would stay as far away from Woodbridge, Indiana, as his ideas on marriage would stay away from hers.

She harrumphed and pulled her hands apart, realizing too late that her fingers still had a tight grip on the bootie.

Ching. Ching. Kaching. The metal hit the concrete at her feet, then began to bounce down the steps in a wild zigzagging motion.

Becky groaned. She should have known something like this would happen, especially on a rotten day like this. She turned, trying to tuck the wild confusion of curls dangling along one side of her face back into the comb that now hung at the nape of her neck. Her lower lip trembled, but she made herself stave off the pitiful crying jag building up within her. Time enough for that later, she thought, for now she ought to at least try to find the charm. She sighed and clomped down the church steps, her head bent as she scanned the area for a silver speck among the scattered birdseed. The soft seeds crumbled beneath her feet, mashing into the soles of her shoes, a stray seed occasionally popping up to bounce against her ankle. When one ricocheted inside her shoe, she cursed under her breath and plunked herself down on the bottom step in order to remedy the problem.

A couple passing by the church cut a wide berth to walk around where she was sitting. That suited her well as it meant they were less likely to kick or trample her charm if it had fallen on the sidewalk. For all she knew, though, it could have taken a wayward skip and landed in the bushes or dropped in a pile of seed and sunk into it.

"Durned old birdseed. Stupid town ordinance," she muttered. She slipped her shoe from her foot, wriggling her toes against the concrete to try to free the errant seed from her stocking. She did it, too, by straining so hard she poked her big toe through the end of her ninety-nine-cent panty hose. She pinched the hole closed. A huge run tripped its way up over her foot and all the way to her shin. "Crummy hose."

She heard more approaching footsteps, but she didn't care. She hadn't had such a lousy day since that morning when she'd gone job hunting in the rain with her crooked glasses on, lost her charm and met a prince in a power suit. And look how *wonderfully* that all turned out, she mused. All started off by the same commonplace little charm that she'd lost today.

Shoe in her lap, she took one last, slow survey of the seed-dappled sidewalk. "Darn that charm anyway. I'll probably never see it again. And as long as I'm cussing out things I'll never see again—"

"Is *this* what you're looking for?" A pair of familiar Italian loafers stopped directly in front of her.

Becky stared at the gleaming trinket held before her eyes by strong, masculine fingers with neat but not manicured nails. She dared not move. She dared not hope it could be him. How could it be?

Her heart raced. Her mind refused to focus on anything. She started to warn herself not to hope for too much, not to let herself get caught up in another useless dream, but she cut herself off. She *would* hope. If Clark had come to her, that alone would be proof enough that not all her dreams were foolish fantasies.

Taking a deep breath, she looked up. "Oh, my word! It *is* you! You're really here."

He knelt, placed the charm in her cupped hand, then curled her fingers shut around it. "In the nick of time, I hope."

Her eyes met his. "Clark."

He smiled. "Yes."

If this was the closest she ever got to a dream coming true, Becky decided in that split second it would be enough. Unable to hold back her joy, she tucked the charm into her pocket, then threw her arms around him, not caring as her shoe tumbled to the ground. She pressed her cheek to his neck and inhaled deeply the scent of him, savored the heat of his body and flattened her hands against his muscular back.

She closed her eyes, her lips brushed his warm skin, and she became wildly aware of his steady, hard pulse even as she murmured, "You're here. You're here. You're really here."

"I'm here," he whispered. One hand supported her as she leaned toward him, and with the other he stroked the loose, full curls away from the side of her face.

"You are here," she said, pulling away so that she could see him, her hand on his cheek out of fear this possible figment of her overly active imagination might suddenly vanish if she let go. "You're here in

Woodbridge and...*why* are you here in Woodbridge?"

"I came to stop the wedding." Quiet passion gripped his tight tone.

"The...?" She cocked her head. She certainly hadn't seen that answer coming.

He said nothing, just gazed into her eyes with solemn expectation.

Confused and probably a bit in shock over his sudden appearance and this peculiar mission, she blinked at him, then said, "Um, if you've come to stop the wedding, you're too late."

"I am?" His naturally dark complexion went ashen.

"Yes." She felt herself nod though she hadn't planned to. "But if you hurry over to the VFW hall, you still have time to make an insulting toast to the bride and groom, if that will make you feel any better."

"The bride and groom? Aren't you the bride?"

"Me? You have got to be kidding! *Me?*" She laughed so hard her movements shook the hair comb down another two inches in her tangled hair and more curls plopped onto her back and shoulders. She shifted her feet, one foot wearing a shoe, the other sporting a whole new meaning for the open-toed look. "Honestly, Clark, do I look like a bride to you?"

She sat back on the step, holding both her arms out so that he could see her in all her glory.

He took a long, lingering look, then a smile broke slowly across his lips. "You look wonderful to me."

She sighed, probably even blushed; she wasn't quite sure. "I look a mess, but I'll take the compliment and return it tenfold. It's so good to see you again and to hear you say...you came to *stop* the wedding?''

Still kneeling on the sidewalk at her feet, he took her hand. ''Well, I couldn't very well let you marry Frankie McWurter, could I? Not without a fight at least.''

''You and Frankie, now there's a fight that they'd sell tickets to as the mismatch of the century—second only to a match of Frankie and me getting married.'' Becky shook her head as she thought of such a thing. ''Where did you get a crazy idea like that anyway?''

''Let's say a little bird told me. A little bird with a crumpled-up twenty-dollar bill in her beak.'' He arched an eyebrow.

Becky moaned and shut her eyes. ''Mrs. Mendlebaum! I told her to leave that money with someone in your office. Don't tell me she wangled her way in to see you instead—and plied you with some phony story about me getting married?''

''She swore she heard you say yes to a Saturday wedding.''

''As a guest.''

''Her intentions were good.'' He turned over her hand in his, then covered it with his other hand.

''Her intentions were to meddle.'' She placed her free hand on top of his, as well.

''And for this you're objecting?'' he said in a perfect imitation of her neighbor, the good-hearted busybody.

Becky laughed. She hadn't laughed in so long she'd forgotten how truly wonderful it felt. ''No, I'm not objecting. I'm just...well, I am curious. When we last saw each other, we'd reached a serious impasse. It didn't seem as if we had any kind of future if one of us didn't—"

"Grow up a little?"

"Yes." She bit into her lower lip. Her fingers traced his long fingers. "Your coming here like this, Clark, it says so much to me. It's all I really wanted from you, you know, a sign that you could compromise, that you were willing to try to work on our differences regarding our relationship and our future. Now that you're here, I have that sign. But I need to hear it from you. I need to know why you came, why you went to this great length to stop me from marrying another man."

"I came because..." He paused and a peculiar look crossed his face. He slipped one hand from her grasp and pressed his fist high against his chest. "You wouldn't happen to have any of those antacids on you anymore, would you?"

She suppressed the giddy flutter in her own stomach and shook her head. If he'd actually said the three little words to her, Becky didn't think she could feel any happier. "No, I don't have any antacids, but according to Mrs. M, they won't do you any good anyway."

"Mrs. M?" He chuckled, winced, then chuckled again, this time doing it carefully, as though trying not to jar his body too much. "Oh, wonderful. First she knows what's best for us romantically and now she's a health-care specialist."

"Let's combine the two and call her a heart specialist." She reached out to caress his angular jawline with her palm. "She told me her husband Chester used to get pains just like the ones you're experiencing now. She told me it's how a man feels when he can't admit he's in love. It only goes away when he does admit it and then does something about it.''

"Is that so?"

"That's what Mrs. M says." Becky couldn't bring herself to fully endorse the idea, not without the risk of scaring Clark off again. He'd come to her, shown her he was now open to change; she didn't need anything more today.

"Well, if Mrs. Mendlebaum says that's the only cure for what ails me, then I say it's time to take my medicine." He smiled, his chin lowered so that he had to look up at her with those mesmerizing eyes. His gaze never moved from hers as he slid his hand into his pocket and pulled out a tiny jewelry box like the one he'd given her the repaired bootie in and the one he'd had at Rosemont House.

"Oh, Clark, another charm to mark this momentous occasion for me. You shouldn't have."

"I didn't."

"What? But you—"

"Shhh. This is not the kind of thing I ever planned on doing. I certainly would hate to have to do it over because you weren't listening the first time."

Her heart stopped. She tried to blink or swallow, but she had no idea if she accomplished either.

"Rebecca Taylor, I love you. I think I loved you from the very first day I saw you all bedraggled but fearless, proud yet vulnerable. I know I loved you the day you helped with that perfume negotiation when you showed how smart and capable you are, and later at the Pork and Pins when you proved to me you weren't out after my money or status. I think if I had let myself admit it, I loved you even more then. And when I kissed you—''

"I loved you, too, right from the start, even though I tried to tell myself it was only a fantasy, that it couldn't really be true or come true." She scooted to the edge of the step, drawn closer to him with his every word and her every kindred emotion. "Girls like me, from small towns and poor families, without a college degree or a high-powered job, we just don't fall in love with men like you, not and have that love returned. It seemed too much to hope that I could be the one to find a prince.''

"A prince?" Laughter shone in his eyes.

"Like Cinderella," she explained.

"Ah," he said, nodding. "That's a good analogy."

"You think?" she croaked out, still a little amazed at herself for confessing it.

"Yes, I do." He leaned in, his lips teasing the soft skin beside her ear as he whispered, "Because in the end, if I remember my fairy tales correctly, Cinderella marries her prince.''

She pulled back. "M-marries?"

"I'm not afraid of it anymore, Becky. When I thought of what it would be like to live my life without you, I realized that we're not like my parents and we're not going to turn out like them. That was then—old business. It's done and behind me now. What's ahead of me is you, the two of us building a life and home and family together, if you'll have me." He held out the small box, lifting its hinged top up with one hand until a brilliant diamond solitaire winked out at her from a bed of black velvet. "Rebecca Taylor, will you marry me?"

"Oh, yes, Clark, I will. I will."

Even as she said the words, he slid the ring onto her finger. A perfect fit sealed by a perfect kiss. And then another. And another.

Without knowing how, Becky found herself standing on the steps, the sun on her back, her hair comb clattering down to scatter the birdseed on the sidewalk and Clark's arms wound tightly around her. She felt his heartbeat thudding against her full breasts, his taut thigh muscles tensing as they pressed to hers and every nuance in between. Smiling, she pulled her lips away from his to murmur, "Oh, Clark, I think we ought to go someplace and celebrate this."

"I'm all for that, but there are a couple of little loose ends we need to see to first."

Becky scowled. "Loose ends? What?"

"This." He slid from her arms and took a step to retrieve the shoe that had fallen from her lap. With a flourish, he bent his knee again, then placed his hand on her heel and deftly guided her foot into the shoe. "There you go, Cinderella."

"Thanks." She grinned and gave him a wink and he rose and offered her his arm. "You're a prince."

He gave her a quick but genuinely knee-weakening kiss, then began to lead her toward his car, parked just across the quiet street.

"You said there were a couple of loose ends we needed to take care of," she reminded him as they strolled to the car. "My shoe was one. What's the other?"

"We're going to stop at a jewelry store and get

that bootie welded onto your charm bracelet,'' he answered, then kissed her nose.

She laughed with a lightness of heart she'd never even dreamed of and then gave him a sultry smile. ''And *then* we're going to celebrate?''

''Happily, and forever after,'' he promised.

Chapter Twelve

"Clark? Remember when we eloped and I said I thought we should celebrate our first anniversary by having a real wedding? A big blowout with the dress and cake and everything?"

Clark held his wife's hand, his mind not fully on what she was saying. "Uh-huh."

"And you said no, you'd rather we went on a real honeymoon instead—a cruise, a romantic hideaway, maybe show me Europe and the Greek Islands?"

He touched her face, not sure what she was trying to tell him or why she had picked this time to do it. "Vaguely, yes."

"Well, I've decided that's what I want to do."

"Which?"

"Either one. Or why not both? Let's pack our bags now, or better yet, forget the bags. We'll buy whatever we need when we get there. Let's just go and go now-ow-ow-*ow!*"

"Sorry, my dear, the big travel agent in the sky has made other plans for our anniversary—we're going to spend it in the delivery room. Now breathe."

"I am breathing. How could I be talking if I wasn't bre—hee-hee-hee—" she incorporated the technique into the conversation, then finished the word in a big whoosh of air "—thing."

Clark smiled down at his beautiful wife, made even more beautiful to him now as their love had deepened this past year and in doing so had created this impending miracle. He stroked back the damp curls that had come loose from her ponytail and held her hand against the crisp birthing-room sheets. "You're doing great, honey. All in all, I don't think this is such a bad way to spend our anniversary."

"Easy for you to say." She held his fingers in a viselike grip. "You're not experiencing labor pains."

"I would if I—"

"Don't," she warned.

"All right, so it's trite," he admitted as he leaned over her, using his free hand to wipe the sweat from her brow. "But I hope you know that I would do anything within my power to protect and keep you from pain, Becky. You mean more to me than I ever thought another person could. I love you and it's torturous for me to see you going through this and not be able to do anything but stand here and coach."

"I know." She reached up to lay her hand against his neck. "If it helps, you can think of this less as hard labor and more as a way for me to earn three new charms for my bracelet."

"Three?"

"Breathe, Clark, breathe," she said, turning the

coaching technique on him. "Two for the babies, one for our anniversary—I think this qualifies as a memorable one, don't you?"

"Yes, I do. I do," he commented, laughing. "Absolutely I do."

"Gee, everything I went through to get you to say those two little words and now I can't get you to stop."

"How we doing in here?" A cheery-faced nurse popped into the softly decorated room.

"You and I seem to be holding up quite well, but my wife is in a lot of pain," he told her in a strong mix of sarcasm, humor and edgy concern. "When will the doctor be in?"

"I came to tell you he's just arrived and will be here in a minute. It won't be long now." She patted Becky's shoulder, then turned on her thick-soled heel to walk away. After only a few steps, she looked back. "Oh, I almost forgot. There's a man and a woman here. They say they're family. Their last name is—"

"Mendlebaum?" Clark glanced at Becky, realized she'd begun another contraction and closed in at her side. His focus on his wife, he managed to call out to the nurse. "Tell them I'll let them know as soon as the babies get here."

"Clark," Becky gasped out.

"Breathe," he coached. "Find your focal point and blow out in short, quick puffs. You remember how."

"I...have...to...tell...you...something." She used the short, controlled breaths to get the message out.

"Can't it wait?" He clenched his teeth as he watched her struggle through the peak of the contractions, then relax as the strain in her body began to ease up.

When she'd exhaled a long, weary sigh, his darling wife looked up at him. "I just thought you might want to know ahead of time. I promised Mrs. M that if we have a girl, I'd name it after her."

"That only seems fair," he said, smiling. After what she'd gone through, he'd let her name the babies anything she wanted—within reason. He crimped his brow down, suddenly needing a little assurance and information. "And if one or both of the twins is a boy?"

"I talked her out of Chester for a boy."

Clark said a silent thank-you.

"You know, sometimes in order to make the people you love happy, you have to learn to compromise."

Clark smiled, his heart full. "I know, princess, I know."

He bent down to kiss her forehead, but just then an unexpected contraction hit her hard. The doctor came striding into the room, commenting on how close the pains were coming and issuing orders for gowns and masks and gloves and drapes. Instantly all manner of preparations began to bring his children—his and Becky's children—into the world.

Less than an hour later, the happiness he thought could not get any bigger multiplied by two. Then, when he held his identical twin daughters in his arms and gazed down at their mother at his side, it multiplied by ten thousand.

"Welcome to the world, little Chelsea Estelle and Celeste Elizabeth." He cooed to the impossibly tiny beings God had given him as part of the miracle of his loving Becky. His eyes then on his wife, he went on to make a promise that he never believed his battered heart would allow until he met this wonderful woman. "Welcome to a world with two loving parents who will do everything within their power to make sure you always have your very own happily ever after."

He kissed the girls on the forehead, then placed them in Becky's waiting arms, and with a kiss on her lips, he told her that she and the babies had helped to finally make his life complete.

* * * * *

Don't miss Silhouette's newest cross-line promotion,

Four royal sisters find their own Prince Charmings as they embark on separate journeys to find their missing brother, the Crown Prince!

The search begins in October 1999 and continues through February 2000:

On sale October 1999: **A ROYAL BABY ON THE WAY**
by award-winning author **Susan Mallery** (Special Edition)

On sale November 1999: **UNDERCOVER PRINCESS**
by bestselling author **Suzanne Brockmann** (Intimate Moments)

On sale December 1999: **THE PRINCESS'S WHITE KNIGHT**
by popular author **Carla Cassidy** (Romance)

On sale January 2000: **THE PREGNANT PRINCESS**
by rising star **Anne Marie Winston** (Desire)

On sale February 2000: **MAN...MERCENARY...MONARCH**
by top-notch talent **Joan Elliott Pickart** (Special Edition)

ROYALLY WED
Only in—
SILHOUETTE BOOKS

Available at your favorite retail outlet.

Visit us at www.romance.net

SSERW

If you enjoyed what you just read,
then we've got an offer you can't resist!

Take 2 bestselling love stories FREE!

Plus get a FREE surprise gift!

Clip this page and mail it to Silhouette Reader Service™

IN U.S.A.	IN CANADA
3010 Walden Ave.	P.O. Box 609
P.O. Box 1867	Fort Erie, Ontario
Buffalo, N.Y. 14240-1867	L2A 5X3

YES! Please send me 2 free Silhouette Romance® novels and my free surprise gift. Then send me 6 brand-new novels every month, which I will receive months before they're available in stores. In the U.S.A., bill me at the bargain price of $2.90 plus 25¢ delivery per book and applicable sales tax, if any*. In Canada, bill me at the bargain price of $3.25 plus 25¢ delivery per book and applicable taxes**. That's the complete price and a savings of over 10% off the cover prices—what a great deal! I understand that accepting the 2 free books and gift places me under no obligation ever to buy any books. I can always return a shipment and cancel at any time. Even if I never buy another book from Silhouette, the 2 free books and gift are mine to keep forever. So why not take us up on our invitation. You'll be glad you did!

215 SEN CNE7

315 SEN CNE9

Name _____ (PLEASE PRINT)

Address _____ Apt.# _____

City _____ State/Prov. _____ Zip/Postal Code _____

* Terms and prices subject to change without notice. Sales tax applicable in N.Y.
** Canadian residents will be charged applicable provincial taxes and GST.
 All orders subject to approval. Offer limited to one per household.
 ® are registered trademarks of Harlequin Enterprises Limited.

SROM99 ©1998 Harlequin Enterprises Limited

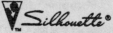

The clock is ticking for three brides-to-be in these three brand-new stories!

3, 2, 1... Married!

In this exciting collection of romantic tales, three marriage-minded women set their sights on becoming brides in time for the New Year.

How to hook a husband when time is of the essence?

Bestselling author **SHARON SALA** takes her heroine way out west, where the men are plentiful...and more than willing to make some lucky lady a "Miracle Bride."

Award-winning author **MARIE FERRARELLA** tells the story of a single woman searching for any excuse to visit the playground and catch sight of a member of "The Single Daddy Club."

Beloved author **BEVERLY BARTON** creates a heroine who discovers that personal ads are a bit like opening Door Number 3—the prize for "Getting Personal" may just be more than worth the risk!

On sale December 1999, at your favorite retail outlet.

Only from Silhouette Books!

Visit us at www.romance.net

PS321

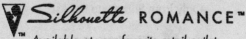